Th...
comp...
about f...
fear. Five girls
become friends whilst
working together.
What could possibly
go wrong?

Signing
OFF
Written by
Janet Easton
Bowsher

About the Author.

This is the first book written by Janet. She is married to Simon and they live in Petersfield, Hampshire, UK.

For further information please go to
http://www.signingoff-thebook.com

Follow on twitter **@JEastonBowsher**

ISBN :- **978-0-9574883-0-4**

Published by Janet Easton Bowsher.

The right of Janet Easton Bowsher to be identified as the author of this work has been asserted to her in accordance with the Copyright, Designs and Patents Act 1988.

Acknowledgements.

Special thanks to Simon, Zara, Celia, Sally and Bruce for their invaluable help.

Also thanks to Helen, Anne, Tanya, Suzanne, Fiona, Claire and Vanessa.

Signing Off.

Debbie

I will always remember the first day in my new job. It was the day I met the friends who changed my life. It was also the day I first felt a sense of foreboding. Of course I was nervous that morning. Mum and Dad never knew; I can appear to be calm and in control at breakfast. As I was driving into work, my stomach churned and my palms were sweaty. I wondered if other people got this anxious, as I tried to regulate my breathing. I swerved into the car park and looked over at the queue of people forming near the main entrance. They must be all the people waiting to sign on. Why had I applied for this job? Who in their right mind would want to work in a job centre?

I fumbled with my bag getting out of the car and headed for the staff entrance. I needed the loo again! Ridiculous! Keep calm. Someone appears at the door, in response to my buzzing. He looks young, vague and disinterested. "Hi" he managed. "Are you one of the new ones then? Didn't they give you the code?"
I showed him the letter and he smiled.
"So, they're throwing you in at the deep end! Still Lyn's ok. Follow me; I'll take you down there."
In a few turns of the corridor, we arrived in a vast open plan office. There seemed to be loads of people, mainly all engrossed in their own computer screens. There was an underlying buzz of peoples' voices mixing with a

continual ringing of phones. A tallish dark haired woman with a big smile was walking towards us with an outstretched hand. She had sparkling vivid green eyes and a warm friendly face.

"Hello, I'm Lyn - the Team Leader of this section." she said above the noise.

I shook her hand quickly and replied "I'm Debbie".

I decided that Lyn seemed quite nice. She asked me about my old job and I joked about how different it was to this place, but she reassured me that there were other new people starting today and that we would get a lot of help. Lyn was a bit older than me - maybe in her early thirties, but the others to whom I was soon introduced, were more my age. Stella was young, with short spiky blond hair, blue eyes and very cool clothes. I noticed she had several charity bracelets on one wrist and a fun chunky watch on the other.

Pippa was also really cool, but a bit superior somehow and I thought her shoulder length wavy blonde hair looked dyed. Her brown eyes were quite heavily made up and flicked over you as if assessing you when you spoke. She was also quite tall like Lyn. Then finally there was Kate - well - how I wished I could be that confident! Although Kate wasn't as pretty or striking looking as the other three, she seemed to have a great sense of humour and a carefree attitude that I immediately envied and admired.

Lyn gave us a guided tour around the building and I was pleased to have a chance to nip into the loo. Apparently there were eighty plus people working here - eight sections on two floors. In my old job there were only ten of us, in total. We were all going to be on Lyn's section - the front line she called it.

I was so glad I wasn't the only new person and almost quite excited that fate had landed me with a group of girls my own age! Maybe we would even become friends. I was already imagining describing them to Mum and Dad and picturing their interest. In my last job, I was the only youngster there. Perhaps that is why I had stuck it for so long - I was safe and protected.

Lyn showed us where our desks were, but explained that for the first few weeks, we would be sat alongside colleagues and would also spend some time in the training room. Discussion around Pippa's last job, made me realise that she knew some of the procedures and had actually just transferred from another job centre site, the other side of the city. Maybe that explained her confidence. Kate seemed to share this confidence though, whilst at least Stella seemed more like a new girl. As I was analysing them all, I realised that at least I had stopped feeling so nervous.

Following a while in the training room, Lyn announced it was time for a break. She took us to the tea room and proceeded to instruct us in the kitchen protocol.
"Very important that you don't use these mugs or take stuff from this cupboard… if you pay into the tea club, you can always use *this* tea, coffee and sugar and then milk *only* from the bottom shelf of the fridge."
The fridge looked as though it hadn't been cleaned in weeks but Kate just laughed loudly and announced

"I suppose there would be a mega problem if you used the wrong milk!"
I smiled; Kate seemed such a laugh.

The aroma of coffee mingled with a vague smell of stale chips, dirty crockery was piled up in the sink and the kitchen surfaces had several dubious looking stains, more suited to a student house rather than an office kitchen. I took in a hand written Out Of Order sign on the front of a dishwasher and a very old and dirty microwave right next to a newer smaller shinier version. I wondered why the old one hadn't been thrown out. Lyn ushered us into the adjoining room, where several other people were congregating around small cheap looking tables. Pippa led us to a free table in the far corner of the room. This would become our table.

Whilst the others chatted, I viewed the rest of the room, surreptitiously. There was quite a mix of ages and types of people. I was sure that our group was being surveyed and dissected. In a moment of complete clarity, I knew this did not matter to me. Conversely, I was delighted - I was part of this group, which was the cause of discussion. Lyn had chosen to sit with us and was chatting about various pubs and cafes, located near the office.
"Anyone got any plans for lunch time?" she asked.
It was apparent that we were all keen to go out somewhere together, so Lyn arranged that we would sample the local pub.

The local was literally a two minute walk away and our pub lunch was cheap and cheerful. Again, I had the sense that other people were looking over at us and wondered if

any of them came from the same office. Lyn and Pippa led most of the conversation. It transpired that Pippa owned her own flat – even though she was only twenty five - the same age as me. She chatted dismissively about her boyfriend Gary and how she wanted to stay single for a good while yet. Instinct told me to keep quiet - they would probably think I was a freak, for never having had a boyfriend. Lyn joked about being past it and an old married woman, when Stella joined in for the first time. She mused, almost to herself;
"Well as long as you are happy - that's the main thing."

The hour we had off for lunch, went by in a flash and we were soon back in the training room. During the afternoon, Lyn brought in the Manager to meet us. Pete seemed very young to be a Manager - not much older than us, but appeared to be slightly shy, which immediately endeared me to him. He explained that he was in charge of three sections on one floor and that Dawn was in charge of the other. Pete didn't seem at all like a boss, he was unassuming, friendly and funny. There was also a big boss, a Senior Manager, called Jerry. Over the weeks that followed, I was to learn that Jerry was considered to be a bit of a joke, but that most people respected Pete and Dawn.

When I arrived home, Mum and Dad asked me about the job, generally, but didn't seem that interested in Lyn, Pippa, Kate, Stella or Pete. I'm sure that after an initial few minutes of discussion, their attention returned to the TV, as ever. I had never really been able to talk to Mum and Dad that much - somehow it felt that I was the odd one out three's a crowd or something like that. I felt a bit deflated, so I went upstairs to my room and opened up my laptop. I started to type down my thoughts about the day. It was Kate that intrigued and probably impressed me the most. She wasn't that cool like the others and I supposed her unremarkable appearance was similar to my own - average height, average build, short mousy brown hair and a forgettable face. Kate though, hadn't seemed fazed by anything or anyone and I was in awe of her arrogant self - belief which I so woefully lacked.

My earlier sense of foreboding had abated, but still niggled at me somewhere at the back of my mind. What could go wrong? I forced myself to think about the positive things that had happened during the day. I thought about the fact that I may be making friends. I decided to keep a journal from then on, about my new found friends. Then I flicked through Facebook - was it too early to friend request them, I wondered?

Lyn.

When I finally got home, following a quick shopping trip after work, I was dismayed to find Rich wasn't there. I knew he loved his job with the Police, so I shouldn't resent the extra hours he put in, compared to my job. Maybe it would be better if I was happier in my work, but that would mean looking for another career. I knew I had stayed put with the job centre for all the wrong reasons - flexi time, pension, being able to walk to work and of course, friends. Thinking about it, that was probably the main reason – we had such a laugh. There had always been some right weirdoes; staff and public, but I had made some really good friends.

I still went out socially with a group of mates, who had started with me, at least eight or nine years ago, but one by one they had all moved into different jobs. In the meantime, of course I had been promoted and that meant more money. I know Rich wants me to stay; thinking that it's something to which I could go back, after having had children. That was something for the future though; what about now?

I began to think about the new girls who started today. Seemed like a really good bunch, actually. Also, I thought they should cope ok with the public and everything. I supposed it was very early days yet, but I could usually tell the ones who would get stressed out. Debbie who seemed quite shy was the only one I had slight reservations about, but I didn't want to judge them too quickly.

Having had security guards in for the last few years, the tension had eased off somewhat and we weren't calling the Police in every other week, like the old days. Of course the memory of first meeting Rich five years ago brought a smile to my face. He had attended one of our regular incidents with another copper and had dragged some guy out kicking and screaming, who wasn't getting his benefit. Unusually, I had actually been pretty frightened at the time, as I was sure this one had some psychiatric problems, as well as the anger. Rich had come back later the same day, to take a statement. I was just so pleased to see him again and I registered the excitement gradually building, as we chatted. He was very easy going, a good laugh, but also kind and considerate - unlike a lot of the previous police guys I had dealt with. The rest as they say was history and we were married about three years later.

"Hey babe" I heard Richard call.
"Hi Rich - I'm glad you're home." I started telling him about the new girls straight away.
"How long do you think they will last then?" he asked.
"Don't know" I replied "but hopefully for a while"

Rich looked at me quizzically.
"Does anyone actually enjoy working there?" I paused before answering. I knew I could cope with the job better than a lot of the others, but was that because I had just become accustomed to it and accepted the crap, because I was pragmatic and didn't want to rock the boat?
"I think most of us just put up with it" I began. "All the petty rules and regulations, ridiculous amounts of checks, paperwork and all that would be ok if we had enough staff to cover everything - but as it is we still keep the public

waiting and then when they kick off, it's a bit of a vicious circle. Added to which it's really hard to try and motivate your staff, when you don't feel valued yourself and you agree with half of what they're complaining about."

"Well you've got these extra staff now" Rich returned "they should help."
He was right, but I knew it would take a bit of time. However, I had a good feeling about the new girls. If nothing else, I felt we shared the same sense of humour and it would be good to have a laugh again, at work. Although I still went out with the friends I had made, when I first started in this office, it wasn't the same as when we had all worked together. The days went by more quickly then and we stifled any stress with good humour and a sense of belonging together. Maybe I would be lucky. Maybe I would return to something similar with this new group.

I supposed I was hoping that work would become more bearable through working with people who were friends, rather than colleagues. It was strange to think that I spent more time with work people, than with friends and family - even Rich. I wondered if it was the same for the majority of people at work - did they feel that they wanted or even needed to be friends with some of their colleagues? I decided that maybe with more career type jobs, it might not be so important. Perhaps there could be value in the actual work? I knew that this was rarely the case with my job.

Rich seemed to enjoy his actual work, as well as having loads of mates, with the Police. He knew he was probably more content than me, and every so often, initiated discussion on me looking for other jobs. Ironically, I think I had stayed put for so long, because of my former friendships and now I thought it would be harder to move on. With my previous friends, time at work had been such a laugh - but of course we had a laugh wherever we were. It was just that we had all initially met at work. Strange, but true, I pondered.

I thought for a while about friendships. I knew I had some good friends from school and from University, but although we all had fairly regular contact, our conversations often reverted to reminiscing. Our meetings had almost become like reunions rather than just nights out. I supposed the difference was that my work friends were more here and now and were sharing the present, rather than the past. I wondered if that over time old work friends would become yet another group like my school or Uni crowd.

Regardless of my introspection, Rich had started kissing my neck and my thoughts of work soon disappeared.

Debbie

Three whole weeks had gone by in my new job. I felt every day had been a bit of an adventure and I looked forward to going to work. The fact that I didn't enjoy the actual work itself didn't bother me too much, but I felt it was almost miraculous that I was part of a group. I was part of a group of friends. How I had yearned for such a position at school. School had been endurance at best and tortuous at worst - the humiliation of petty bullying and the shame of being invisible to most of my peers. Well perhaps all the shyness of my childhood and teenage years were, finally, about to come to an end.

We are all getting on so well, that we have arranged to meet tonight at a pub in town. Naturally, I am nervous, but I am also pretty excited. I wonder what they all think of me. I'm sure they think I'm quiet, but then there's never a gap in any of the conversations! We have fallen into a routine at work, where we try and spend breaks together and always sit at the same table in the tea room. Pippa announced recently that other people were frightened to sit in our seats, Kate had snorted in agreement, but Stella remarked that she didn't really think we were "that scary".

I supposed that I was well out of my comfort zone, but it was worth it. This was all I wanted - friends and a purpose in life. Living and not observing life.

I was worried about what I should wear for the evening out. Clothes for work had to be smart / casual and I felt I could fit in, fairly unobtrusively, with that. Pippa had talked about going clubbing later, which I guessed meant that they may be dressing up - but I really didn't know. They weren't to know that this was all completely new to me. The School Prom and two college parties were the only places I had been to of any comparison and my memories of those were not good. Of course I had never been in with the in crowd and such events had been a trial, rather than something to be enjoyed.

Pippa and Stella were both so lively and so pretty that I was actually in awe of them. Although Lyn was less obviously attractive, she still had lovely sparkly green eyes that contrasted with her thick dark hair. Kate wasn't as good looking as the others - I struggled to picture her clearly when thinking about them at home, but what was really remarkable was the sheer force of her personality. They all shared such a terrific sense of self-worth and confidence though and I could only wonder at how good life could be, if you allowed nothing to stress or worry you.

At least the majority of my school year had become my Facebook friends, which I hoped gave me some credibility. I'm not even sure if I have spoken to all of them, but everyone wants to up their number of friends. It was ridiculous though, because obviously they weren't really friends at all. Of course Miss Social Pippa with her six hundred plus friends probably was good mates with half of hers. Still at least she had accepted my request, along with the others.

As I rifled through my wardrobe, I decided that I must buy some new clothes. I eventually settled for a pair of smart black trousers and a bright red top and surveyed myself in the mirror. I was thinking that I didn't look all that bad, but my reflection scowled back at me. I had darkish rings under my eyes from not sleeping well and these along with a few spots were made more apparent by my pale complexion. Why couldn't I smile? I knew that I was the sort to melt into the background with my average height, mousey short hair and pale, drawn, uninteresting face. No breasts to speak of and thin without being cool. The complete opposite in all things to someone like Pippa! I forced a grin of sorts and took a deep breath.

I decided I had to make more effort to fit in to be accepted in a group of friends. So far in my life, this had never really happened. I supposed I had stayed safe at school, by avoiding the worst bullies, but ensuring I wasn't noticed much either. Of course I didn't intervene when others were set upon. I didn't understand the reasons particular girls were picked on - they were too pretty or too ugly, too bright or too stupid. So at least I hadn't been a complete victim, but I had become adept at being invisible. The isolation had become ordinary and natural for me, but now I felt I had a chance. A chance to have friends! Kate, Pippa, Lyn and Stella were all so bubbly and outgoing - the sort of group that were always having fun and unaware of the attention they attracted. Could I ever really be a part of that? I didn't want to stay as an observer all my life.

As I got in the car, I was thinking that I had a good excuse not to drink. This was another worry for the future - I had never really drunk much alcohol and I was nervous about how it might affect me. However, by offering Stella a lift, I knew I could stick to soft drinks, without anyone

16

questioning me. Stella was the only one who lived on my side of town and like me still lived with her parents. As I arrived outside her house, I beeped the horn twice. The house looked pretty big - but then it would in comparison to our little three bed semi.

Stella came running towards the car.
"I hope I didn't keep you waiting" she said as she got in. Stella started to tell me about her rush to get ready. She explained that she had a younger sister and brother and another older brother who had recently left home. Apparently they all shared a bathroom, which was a constant source of arguments, because their parents' en suite was strictly off limits. However, she was laughing when relaying most of this to me and I thought life would be so much easier in bigger families.
"You are lucky." I said. "I'm an only child"
"Well I bet your parents spoil you rotten, though" she replied.

I was a bit surprised, but tried not to let it show. Surely Stella was just joking, but I felt Mum and Dad weren't that interested in me, because I was on my own and didn't amount to much. They were probably disappointed that they couldn't have any more kids; probably too old. Stella started asking me if I had ever thought of leaving home. I hadn't, but pretended it was something I was planning to do, soon. She chatted on happily about her family and it appeared that they all got on really well. However, she also said that she wanted her independence and had been saving money over the last year or so, with a view to being able to afford her own flat.

"Pippa is really lucky to have her own place already, isn't she?" Stella asked. Earlier on in the week, Pippa had explained that she now owned the flat that she had previously owned jointly, with a former boyfriend. Kate had seemed a bit envious of this, at the time, but Stella had said "good on you" and had proceeded to quiz her about mortgage repayments and other such things. Lyn and Richard of course had a mortgage - but that was different - being a bit older and a married couple. I knew that property prices had been coming down a bit, with the recession, but I still thought it would be impossible to afford anything on our wages and on your own, but didn't say anything to Stella.

I felt Stella looking over at me whilst I continued to drive. "That's a nice top" she said.
I wondered if she was just trying to be nice to me, because she felt sorry for me. I couldn't bear to think that anyone pitied me. If only I could join in, more. If only I was cool, like the rest of them. If only I had more confidence. If only.

As I was parking the car, Stella said
"You must let me drive next time." A chink of hope - that there could be a next time.
Almost immediately accompanied by some stress though, this meant I would have to drink. We walked together into the crowded pub. I squinted to try and see the others, but Stella was ahead of me.
"Hiya and who wants a drink?" she shouted.
"No - let me get yours, as I've already got these in." Lyn replied.

I sat down in an empty chair next to Pippa, wondering how the evening would progress and hoping that I would be a part of it.

Pippa.

Having had a few drinks in the pub, with the new girls from work, I suggested going on to a club. I really wanted to go to "Shades" as Gary had texted me to say he was there. Lyn was up for it and persuaded the others. I had already decided that I really liked Lyn and she didn't seem at all like a boss. Anyhow, whatever, she was a totally good laugh and seemed to be drinking the others under the table! Before we left the pub, I went into the loos and had a cursory look in the mirror. I couldn't help thinking "looking good girl!" and smiled at my reflection. I guess at least I appreciated that I was, like, lucky with my looks.

We wandered down a couple of streets, until we saw the queue forming outside Shades.
"This better be worth it" said Stella "I'm getting cold."
I pushed her in reply and said "Don't be such a wimp!"
I had a quick look at my phone to flick through my messages and before too long we were at the front of the queue. The bouncers soon let us in. They knew me, of course, and I'm sure one of them thought I was really fit. Not that he would get anywhere, poor sod! I strode through the entrance hall and my eyes soon adjusted to the dimly lit club. I swayed a little to the music, as I made my way through to the bar, where I hoped Gary would be.

Although I had had several drinks in the pub, I was keyed up and ready for more. Somehow, Lyn was ahead of me again and trying to attract the attention of the bar staff. I couldn't see Gary immediately, but knew he would be around somewhere.

Lyn was passing drinks back, when I was grabbed from behind.

"Hello gorgeous" Gary smirked.

After a few cursory introductions, we slipped off for a dance. I loved dancing with him. I loved the way loads of other girls and even some blokes, kept looking him over. Even I had to admit that he was indeed very tasty, but he'd have to be, to be with me, wouldn't he?!!

After a few more drinks, Gary suggested moving on.

"Let me just say goodbye to the girls" I said.

I saw that they were surrounded by a group of lads and that poor Debbie looked petrified! I supposed that it was a shame that she was driving – she needed something to stop her being so uptight. Anyhow I was more interested in Gary and the lads they were with looked pretty harmless, so off we went. I smiled at Gary and asked "Your place or mine?"

Before we got to the cloakroom though, I heard Stella shrieking after us. "Hey Pippa!! Where do you think you are going?"

I smiled at her and then over at Gary.

"Why, what's up? You missing me already?"

"Yeah right" she replied "We've only just got here and Debbie wants to go home!"

"Oh my God and so not my problem" I laughed "See you losers at work on Monday."

Walking back with Gary, I thought a bit about the girls. They seemed ok and didn't follow the usual pattern of competing with me for attention from the guys. All through my life I reckon I had dealt with more than my fair share of jealous type girlfriends but my new friends didn't seem like that at all. I tried to think back to a time when I was last single - had to be a few years ago. No matter that no bloke ever quite lived up to my expectations, I knew that would change one day and I sure was going to enjoy myself until then! Life's too short and all that and you're only young once! The crap some people spouted about work /life balance cracked me up too. I thought that if you could have a laugh at work and make the best of things, then what did it matter?

Gary asked me about the girls, letting me know he thought Stella was "quite fit", but I knew that he really wanted to know what they thought about him.
"You are so totally superficial" I chided him. "You've just got a thing about blondes, haven't you babe?"
The conversation didn't continue though as Gary started kissing me. Come to think of it we never talked that much and as usual his tongue was halfway down my throat - never any subtlety! I reckoned we wouldn't have much of a relationship without the sex, but that more than made up for anything else. He so turned me on!

Gary was vain and a bit arrogant, but then he was pretty good looking and I wasn't that self - absorbed not to see the irony. Yeah I guess we were a good match, for now, anyhow.

Debbie

I was dreading the first tea break on Monday morning, after our Saturday night out. Stella had been really sweet about leaving when I had asked her, but no doubt Kate and Pippa would think I was pathetic. Pippa going off early, of course, was acceptable, because she was with a bloke. Anyway, expectation is always worse than the actuality - I must remember this! Frankly, not much was mentioned about the club. Only Stella teasing Lyn that she should be ashamed of herself, for flirting with young guys, what with her being an old married woman and all!

Lyn proceeded to ask us all who we thought was fit. Kate started off, derisively, as ever, saying
"Well, certainly no-one in this building that I've seen so far!"
We all laughed.
Stella said tentatively "What about Johny upstairs?"
"He's gay" shrieked Lyn "Isn't it obvious?"
"I did wonder" Stella replied "but what a waste!"
Pippa looked up "What about Pete? He's not bad looking. Pretty fit actually. Is he single?"
I was quite taken aback that she may be interested in him - I liked him! Also what about Gary - he was her boyfriend wasn't he? Surely, Pete wasn't her type - he was too quiet and too nice!
"I don't think he's got a girlfriend" volunteered Lyn "but then office romances can be a bit dodgy, don't you think?"
Kate studied Pippa and asked her
"Or are you just planning on sleeping your way to the top?"

I couldn't believe what I was hearing! I couldn't believe the nerve of the girl - to come out with a question, like that. Kate was so direct but didn't she know that she was being completely tactless? However, Pippa didn't seem to mind.

"I don't care about promotion," she replied "but Pete might be a bit of a challenge - he will probably run a mile if I start, like, chasing him!!"

I hoped that meant that she wasn't serious. However, I couldn't possibly contemplate any relationship for myself. I don't suppose I would ever have a boyfriend - after all I had never really had any proper friends, until this job. When I was a teenager, I had convinced myself that having a boyfriend could wait and I had hoped that when I was older and working, I would miraculously have the confidence to talk to boys and it would somehow all work out.

I knew I was different somehow, all through my teenage years. It wasn't just the absence of boyfriends. Other girls laughed and cried with each other, shared stuff and helped each other. No one ever did that with me. Other families seemed different too. I watched people when out shopping in town, or sat in coffee bars. They all talked to each other, they connected and appeared to care about one another. I couldn't remember the last time I had been out with Mum and Dad. Come to that I couldn't think of the last time we had all had a long chat about anything, even. They lived in the lounge watching the television and I lived in my room, on my laptop.

Everyone else on Facebook seemed to have more friends than me, more social life and well, more life. My mind starting spinning out of control – why was I so shy and nervous? Why was I different? Why couldn't people like me? Why didn't people want to be with me? Why couldn't I be normal? Sometimes, I wondered if other people covered up like I did - surely everyone gets scared. Scared of normal things though, I thought. Like flying, spiders or other such phobias. Not frightened of life. Not virtually always scared and waiting for something bad to happen.

Kate.

What a dump. What a fucking awful place.

Well I didn't care too much, it wasn't a bad salary and better than the last place I worked in. I had been in this new job for several weeks now. Working in a job centre was ok most of the time. I supposed that some people would get well stressed out by dealing with some of the stupid punters or clients should I say, but I knew I could handle anything. I didn't buy in to all that rubbish that Lyn spouted about it being "a small minority" and "people being in a difficult situation". No, I reckoned there were a lot of scroungers and I would have to stop myself having a go back! Bring it on, I thought.

Some of the older staff are well weird - staid old spinster types and pervy old men in grubby old fashioned clothes. The younger ones aren't much better and I reckon most of them are already jealous of our little crowd, because I've overheard someone describing us as a clique. Well sod the rest of them. Quite a few gay boys around too, flaunting their sexuality like some badge of honour. Well it doesn't impress me.

Everyone goes right on about the stress and all that but I reckon it's just an excuse for half the staff to skive off sick! First thing in the morning all the supervisors run between each section checking on how many staff haven't turned up and then juggle accordingly to make sure no-one is too short. Trouble is half of the staff don't like moving around, so they all start whinging. Course they particularly don't like coming to our section as we have to see the public all day long for their fortnightly signing on. What a joke that is and all. Proof of them looking for work is what we're meant to ask for but sometimes it seems, well, a bit mean and with the ones fiddling the system, they've got all the answers anyhow. You can't win whatever.

Occasionally I get the chance to catch up on Facebook on my phone when no-one is looking. The Gestapo Management has blocked it on our desktops, which just about sums up this place. Talk about petty bureaucracy! We also have to keep a shit load of paper records, how so *21st century*. Don't know if I can be bothered to stay here too long - there's got to be something better than this Funny Farm!

I wanted to get a job that paid better than this one, but that might take a while. It was ok to be living at home for now because good old Dad and Mum didn't ask for much money from me, but I reckoned it would be good to save up enough, to rent somewhere smart, perhaps right in the centre of town? It would be great to have my own place. Pippa didn't know how lucky she was. Must admit that she got on my nerves a bit; she was so smug all the time.

On the other hand, all the girls are a good giggle and going out in the evening was a right crack. So what if the work was a bit of a drag and the blokes weren't worth a second look. I don't know if Pippa was serious about going after Pete, but I might join in with some flirting if she starts. Keep me amused for a bit, maybe. Don't know what all the fuss was about Gary - he seemed a right poser! Haven't met Lyn's husband yet, but I'm sure he can't be as perfect as is implied. Still long may our new gang continue, must get everyone on a night out again!

Debbie.

I don't know if I'm going to pass my probation. Lyn has had to take over some of my interviews and I completely froze when this awful man kept shouting at me. My new friends all seem so much more confident than me and even joke about the incidents. One of the security guards, Tim, hovered in the background, but that didn't stop the man sneering and banging his fist, again and again, on my desk. Tim even said "Calm down mate" but it was more of a request than a demand and I was left to keep the interview going, embarrassed and humiliated. Lyn always makes out as though it's much better now than it used to be, but that's hardly reassurance; she just makes me feel worse about everything, whatever she says.

Outside of work, I'm not on edge exactly, but I replay everything over and over in my mind, wondering if I should have said something differently or tried to be more involved with conversations. I analyse all my interactions - both with the dreaded customers - but more minutely with the other members of staff - particularly Pippa, Kate, Stella and Lyn.
I supposed if I could talk to Mum and Dad it would help, but they aren't interested and I don't want to burden them with my insecurities. Also, I just can't shake off the feeling that something bad is waiting around the corner.
I don't suppose for a minute that Mum and Dad have even noticed my recent heightened anxiety. Once in a blue moon I will sit with them in the lounge where they sit endlessly watching TV. All the rubbish soaps and some of the reality programmes which they like to moan about.

Their conversation is limited to talking about the TV or Dad asking Mum to make tea. They both work so I don't know why Mum still does everything around the house.

She cleans for other people and then cleans for us. I suppose Dad thinks he works longer and harder in his driver / delivery role, but just to make one cup of tea in an evening? Couldn't he do that - just once? He drives me mad; he expects me to help Mum but never does anything himself. Then Mum pulling the little tables out and putting the coasters out. Nobody is here, only us, why bother?

I know other families aren't like this, I just know it isn't normal to feel like a stranger with your own parents, but the gulf between us just widens. I seek the sanctuary of my room, where I can roam the Internet without their accusing and disappointed eyes searching me. They stopped asking me if I wanted to bring friends home, long before I left school.
I've got to get a life at work - not for the work itself but for the potential friendships and a reason to get up in the morning.

I've found that I wake up in the night worrying about what's going to happen the next day. The noise in the office is relentless, everyone appears a bit frantic and so the general atmosphere always seems tense. On the other hand, every quick tea break I manage to spend with the girls is special with everyone laughing and we often go the local pub or a cafe at lunch time. This is such a novelty for me - to be part of a group, that I couldn't entertain the possibility of leaving this job. I will have to learn to deal with it. I will have to cope with any abuse or whatever else that happens.

Stella.

I had been in my new job for over a month and for most of the time I had really enjoyed myself. Although at only twenty two, I was the baby of the group, I felt I had been accepted on equal terms. However, as yet, there was a major part of my life that my new friends knew nothing about. No big deal and certainly nothing I'm ashamed about, but, well, the time just hadn't been right. Also, of course it was so early days, as yet. This was the first proper job I had had, after leaving University. I had been a sort of office junior on some short term temporary contracts, but had never really become friendly with the other staff who were typically very much older than me. I felt I should be doing something with my Art degree - but also that I should be doing something kind of worthwhile.

I suppose I had led quite a sheltered life, having lived at home whilst at Uni. I was lucky though that I had a close family that cared about me - even though I sometimes wondered if they completely accepted me for who and what I was, now. They probably thought I was just going through a phase and I could so imagine them talking about me with a mixture of amusement, affection and concern. It would be up to me to make them realise that the concern was unnecessary. They could even be hoping that I would make new friends with this new job and that would change things for me - but I knew this would never happen.

I had hoped that working for a job centre would be about helping people and hadn't envisaged the difficult side of dealing with peoples' benefits and sometimes angry jobseekers. Although we were still classed as trainees, we were now all assigned to dealing with the public, most of the day. I felt awkward and inefficient a lot of the time, but hoped that I would get better, once I knew more of what I was doing.

I did feel that having signed on myself for a few months, when I was first out of University that I could understand a bit of how unemployed people felt. You couldn't help but feel you just didn't want to be in a job centre and were somehow a little embarrassed to be there at all. Setting up your claim meant having to agree a contract of what you would be doing to look for work and then you had to keep a load of evidence as proof of your job search. No matter how decent and understanding the member of staff, it was easy to see why some customers felt aggrieved - whether they felt patronised, confused or intimidated by the whole demeaning process.

On the other hand the staff did get a lot of grief from some of the people signing on – quite a bit of which was so totally undeserved. I felt really sorry for Debbie when some bloke just completely lost it, but she was bailed out by Lyn, who came and took over. Lyn calmed him down eventually, but Debbie seemed very quiet for the rest of the day. Lyn seems really good at talking with all the jobseekers - young and old, yobs and posh people. I think maybe her calm and considerate manner works wonders with distressed people and I have listened and learnt a lot from her already.

Debbie didn't look very happy when Pippa was relaying the incident, later, to an audience in the tea room. Pippa was only having a laugh and I'm sure she's actually pretty caring, although I think some of the staff outside our group have already decided that she's a bit arrogant. Anyway, I would not be one to judge, you had to see the best in people. You had to see the potential that everyone had.

Pippa seems good and quick at dealing with customers too, like Lyn, which was in complete contrast to two older and more experienced workers on our section. The man and woman probably both around fifty odd appeared to do everything to avoid doing anything beyond the bare minimum of work and probably only dealt with half the customers that the rest of us did. Maybe it was uncharitable of me to think of them like this, but it bugged me that having worked here longer and being my parent's age, they were in no way setting an example. They really just didn't care and I kind of vowed to myself that I would never end up like them - lazy and cynical.

I wondered what colleagues like this and more importantly my new friends would all think, though, if they knew about my life, outside of work. Although we hadn't known each other for long, I sort of already felt quite close to these new friends and was beginning to wonder how I could open up to them and if our friendship could be a bit threatened as a result.

Debbie.

Lyn took me aside today and we went off into a meeting
room, for a private chat. This was during work time,
though and my mind was racing with uncertainty. She
started by asking me how I thought I was getting on.
"Why what do you think?" I stuttered.
I was actually thinking - I bet you don't bother asking
Stella, Kate or Pippa.
"Well, it's still early days, but I think you're doing really
well and you are very good on remembering all the
procedures" she said.
I was a bit surprised and although my mouth was still very
dry, I did feel slightly less nervous. Perhaps she wasn't
telling me off after all?   Also it was just the two of us and
she had no notes or anything and wasn't writing anything
down - so maybe it was just a chat?

"I know it can be difficult dealing with angry customers"
Lyn continued "but you will get more training on that and
you must come and get me to help out if ever they keep on,
like that prat the other day".
I wasn't sure if she expected me to reply and I didn't know
what to say, so an uncomfortable silence ensued.
Eventually she asked if I was happy with everything, so I
mumbled an assertion. She was looking at me so closely
somehow that I ended up looking away and through the
glass partition back on to the section. Eventually she took
the hint and said
 "Oh well back to work then."

All through my life I had struggled to stick up for myself and had learnt that mostly it was better not to try and get too involved with people. I supposed it was a way of avoiding being hurt, but there was always a price to pay. People like Lyn probably never thought like this - they sailed through life, gaining or discarding friends, as it suited them. If only I could work out if she was going to be a friend to me or not. I decided that I couldn't trust her, any more than someone like Pippa, much as I ached to be part of this group.

For all her platitudes, Lyn seemed to be trying too hard with me. Her reassurances and offers of support were over the top and had probably been trotted out before, I couldn't help thinking.

Maybe this cosy chat was actually the start of Lyn trying to get me to fail my probation. I decided I wouldn't refer anyone to her, no matter how much they shouted. Why would she do this if she was my friend, though? I couldn't stop myself analysing the situation, over and over in my head and I knew I would find it difficult to talk to Lyn again.

Lyn

Although I think I'm quite good at my job, there are times when I wished I didn't have to manage staff. I reflected that most of the time I could read people pretty well, but I found it was really hard talking to Debbie the other day. She obviously found it difficult dealing with a Mr Angry but it was as though she didn't want to admit to needing any help. She's obviously quite a nervous person, but trying to cover that up. I'm not sure what she's thinking, but if anything I feel that she might resent me - but what for? I talked for a while to Rich about it and he reckons she's a bit of a nut case, but maybe I painted the picture too harshly.

Rich is always great at putting things into perspective and making me worry less about work. When we were first together, I hadn't really thought I was ready for a serious relationship, but then we just got on so well and shared so much, whilst still both having a few separate friends and interests. When he proposed two years later I knew that this was the man I wanted to spend the rest of my life with, not just because we had the most fantastic sex, but more because he had actually become my best friend. A best friend and a lover rolled into one had to be the ideal combination and I was mature enough now to appreciate this happiness. I worried sometimes that I had too much of my fair share of happiness and that somehow the scales would be tipped against me in the future, but how ridiculous is that?

Of course I worry about Rich in his job, but he jokes that working in a job centre is far more dangerous than being a policeman! I know he has been in some nasty situations, but he has always made light of it and genuinely doesn't appear to get stressed about anything. I guess that is how people would view me at work - totally calm, easy going and laid back, but actually I have increasingly found it difficult to switch off from work, particularly if there's been an incident with the public or aggro with a member of staff. Maybe I was even getting a bit stressed in my old age of thirty two, as I didn't recall anything much ever bothering me before about work. There had always been the psychos - both sides of the counter (!!) to deal with. On the other hand it was still so good when things went right; it was great helping people to find jobs or even sometimes just connecting with jobseekers who mostly were in a situation they would rather have avoided at all costs.

Anyway the girls have all decided to go out for a pizza on Friday of next week, so I hope that everything goes ok. It took a while to sort out a night when everyone was free and Stella seemed a bit cagey about where she was on some nights, which was a bit strange. They are all good fun though and pretty genuine and I also mustn't worry too much about Debbie. I guess she'll be fine. Maybe if we all have a good laugh at work, the stress will kind of get wiped out. My old friends I had started with at the job centre had been great fun to work with, but they had all left to go to other jobs and none of them had wanted promotion. I smiled as I remembered a conversation between Pete and my friend Becca.
Pete had said

"This could be a real chance for you - temporary promotion would stand you in good stead for the future and the money's much better."

"I don't want to be disrespectful" Becca had replied "but quite honestly Pete; I would rather stand in a bucket of shit than become an Advisor!"

Pete had had the sense to laugh it off.

"I'll take that as a "no" then."

Debbie

I don't know if Lyn has noticed, but I think I'm coping more with dealing with the public now. It helped when Stella confessed that she gets flustered if they start shouting at her. Also, the other day, Jerry the big boss had to come out from his office to see someone and everyone was saying how useless he is with customers. No one seems to have a good word to say about Jerry. Various criticisms have included that he skives off, that he delegates virtually everything to Pete and Dawn and that he has his favourites amongst the Supervisors. I supposed that Lyn was one of these so called favourites, although she runs him down as much as anyone else.

I know I should have felt sorry for one of the Advisors, Nadia, on another section, but I couldn't help being glad that someone else was getting more abuse than I ever had. It was the talk of the tea room that some report had been made and the police had been involved, following a recent incident. Some staff thought that Nadia wasn't very good at dealing with customers but Lyn and Stella were both outraged that the client hadn't been arrested afterwards. The guy had apparently screwed up some paper and threw it at her, calling her a "Paki bitch". He had gone on to say he would find out where she lived and that she had "better watch her back" as he would "get her and make her sorry." Of course he also used lots of swear words.

When I was on my own with Kate she had surprised me by saying she thought it was a lot of fuss about nothing. Apparently she didn't see that there was much wrong with calling someone a "Paki" and didn't see that as being racist, like the others had. She said she agreed with her Dad who thought everyone had to be "so politically correct" that they were frightened to say anything.

I knew a fair few of the Advisors had a lot of problems dealing with the public and that their job was tougher than ours, but the Team Leaders and Managers had the real problem ones referred on to them.
Pete, therefore, seemed really good with the Jobseekers or cool as Pippa would say. He often took difficult angry people off to a private interview room and invariably managed to calm them down. I suppose it is ridiculous for me to even fantasise about Pete, I'm sure he will end up with someone really outgoing like Pippa or maybe Kate. On the other hand they are both so brash and over confident – perhaps they could scare him off. He's quite unassuming and apparently unaware of how good looking he is. Even though he's a Manager, he accepted my recent Facebook friend request which I though was brilliant. However, once I was able to check him out, I could see that most of the office was listed amongst his friends. Tortuous though it has been, I have actually managed to exchange a few words with Pete and this has made all my nervousness about work almost bearable.

Maybe I am getting used to the job and work - although I'm still so anxious coming in each morning and some kind of big dark cloud continues to loom in the background. Even if I don't get to know Pete that well - just being part of a group of friends is all that I've ever wanted. However much I try and convince myself to the contrary though, I still feel like the odd one out.

Kate

Work is still, well, boring, having to do loads of pathetic checks, but at least dealing with the public livens things up a bit. Lyn our so so saintly supervisor, always goes on about how it's just the minority that moan or get angry, but can't she see that no-one's that happy to be signing on? Well, apart from all the ones that are fiddling the system or just plain scroungers and that's quite a few of them, no doubt. So we're left to deal with anger and the lies.

Stella has gone on about enjoying helping people find jobs, but I think most of the ones I see aren't that bothered. Stella seems a bit soft and always makes excuses for people. Then there's Debbie who's a right wimp who won't say boo to a goose!

I think why can't these people do stuff for themselves, anyway? Are we meant to hold their hands all the way to job interviews too? As for trying to get clients off the Sick - well that's another joke. I know my Dad has said half of them have got cash in hand jobs, supplementing their benefit! I reckon he's not wrong, either. Course the nutters or ones with mental health issues should I say, are the worst. How can you prove someone should work if their doctor keeps signing them off with depression or whatever? God, you look at some of these people and you can't help thinking dregs, the dregs of society. It isn't right that we're not even going to get a pay rise this year, dealing with half the people we do.

It's right crazy that they've said there's a ban on recruitment, too. Some crap about having to cut costs and make savings. Hello? So don't Government or whatever understand that unemployment's going up? So we're quite new - we've only been in a few months, but already in that time two staff retired and two have gone to other jobs and they're not being replaced. It's like we're almost considered old hands now and the so-called training is on the back burner. I know that Lyn and Stella have both got degrees, so they should have better jobs than this. What's the point of going to University for three years and then ending up here?

Well I'm going to see how many of the punters I can catch out. I'm going to make them squirm and if I think they are working and not declaring it then I'm going to refer them to the fraud team, no problem! That has got to be one of the best jobs in this dump - at least working on the fraud team you could get some kind of job satisfaction. Almost like being in the Police or something - having a bit of control. Yeah, maybe I could get to work with them after I've been in for a while.

There are always the tea breaks to look forward to, though, when it's not too busy. Our table is the place to be and where the most noise comes from. A few others come and join us from time to time and I reckon a few more would if they had a bit more guts. I knew a lot of the older staff looked down their noses at us, but other youngsters were more envious of the laughs we were having. Some of the others were ok though and joined in with some of the madder conversations.

"Would you sleep with Jerry for a million quid?" was the starting question from Nadia on another table at one of many uproarious times!

A regular game of chucking two bags of crisps around the room - fast and furious till they split can be a right laugh too!

The maddest thing that has happened so far though, has to be the "Phantom Poo-er!" Lyn was virtually crying with laughter as she made us all follow her into the loos. Stella was furiously trying to flush the loo and as we all peered in, we saw a huge turd filling the bottom of the pan - literally the size of a milk bottle!

"I found it like this, honestly it wasn't me!" shrieked Stella.

"Yeah right" laughed Pippa as she got her phone out to take pictures. "Oh My God – and I'm tweeting this right now!"

We all looked down in amazement as others were filing in to see what all the commotion was about.

"I think it might be one of the workmen that have been in here" Lyn said "that can't have come out of one of us surely?"

"One of us, as in women?" asked Stella "I'm not even sure it's human!"

The shit jokes continued on for several days afterwards and we had several bets on potential candidates. Course prissy Debbie didn't join in much but even Pete had a laugh with us over the whole thing. Lyn had to draw him a life size sketch, which looked pretty much like a vacuum flask, as he hadn't been around to witness the original.

Pete quite often comes over to our table to join us, but I was a bit annoyed recently when Pippa made everyone move around so that she could sit by him. Even Lyn tends to flirt a bit with him and all. Probably looking to go from Supervisor to Manager! Pippa then proceeded to hog the conversation, as per usual. Of course she's no doubt looking to become a Supervisor, what a stupid cow. She then starting questioning Pete about his social life and recommended that he should go to some of the bars where she goes! God, she's so obvious, what a slag!

Debbie

I don't suppose Pete has even noticed me. Anyway, I'm convinced now that he fancies Pippa, just like everyone else. Why can't I be more like her? I'm sure Kate was quite peeved when Pete was chatting away to Pippa, but I don't know why she was surprised or angry by it, I can see that it's all inevitable. It's so unfair that your life can be mapped out as easy and wonderful just by being born pretty. I supposed that Pippa had boys and men fighting over her all through her life and expected their admiration.

Pete also seems quite friendly with Lyn, but I thought that may be a management thing. I've noticed that they often speak - just the two of them - after management meetings and seem to be laughing and joking a lot.
However, my immediate worry is our next night out - how will I cope, how will they all treat me, particularly Lyn, and how much should I drink, as Stella has offered me a lift? Stella sometimes seems a bit secretive and I'm not sure what that's all about. I suppose it might help me to relax if I have a few drinks, but I don't know what my reaction may be - as I never had more than two and then have felt a bit out of control. Also I know they would think it really wimpy if I didn't have at least four or five and I've just got to fit in, now.

It's so tough though - often I just don't get the humour - what was so funny about that huge pooh? I just found it disgusting. Still that is only one thing and more than anything I wanted to try and connect with them, I wanted desperately to be accepted and to be their friend.

Stella

Debbie seemed a bit stressed, in the car on our way to the restaurant, so I was the one doing most of the talking. Well chatting away, but really saying nothing. I was wondering what my new friends would think if they knew about my spiritual life - the fact that I was a practising Christian and proud of it. My family remained somewhat bemused by my recent conversion, but I had made lots of new Christian friends, through the Church I had been attending for over two years. Even though I thought my new mates at work were all pretty non- judgemental, I knew this might not be cool to them. I realised now that actually I should have said something straight away, so it wouldn't seem anything out of the ordinary.

Sarah my younger sister was away at University most of the time and Ben out most of the time with his college friends. They never talked much to me anyway about anything serious. Of course when Phil my older brother visited us though, he so couldn't resist teasing me about church, but I felt his dismissive comments only served to strengthen my faith. Mum and Dad wanted me to be happy more than anything else and I had to sort of respect their "each to their own" philosophy of life. The important thing was that they accepted who I was now but I just worried that someone like Pippa and probably the others at work might not understand at all.

Perhaps, more importantly they wouldn't give me time to explain or maybe it would kind of affect our friendship, but I felt that I wanted them to know. I didn't want them to think it was a secret or something that I was ashamed about - quite the opposite. I discussed it with some friends from church and they felt I should be open and honest. Well maybe sometime soon!

I asked Debbie if she had been to the Pizza place we were going to, but she said she hadn't. Sometimes she seems a bit lost and I don't know if it would help her for me to talk about how my life has changed through coming to know Jesus. On the other hand I don't want to single anyone out. I hadn't needed or lacked anything when I had gone to this church with a friend from University - but something had so happened which changed me forever. I didn't want to become preachy or too evangelical as I knew that would put most people off. Looking back I had been very sceptical to start with, but just couldn't deny the wave of faith that gently washed over me and eventually enveloped me in its warmth.

Ideally, I so wanted everyone to share this faith, this love of God, but I was realistic enough to know that for some people it would be a much more difficult or indeed impossible journey. I was hoping my Mum and Dad would start to understand a bit more, but knew they would take a lot of time. I didn't want to get exasperated with them about their own religion, but felt that their annual trips to Church at Christmas were part of a tradition or a routine rather than a genuine faith.

Then maybe a time would sort of come for Sarah and Ben, but probably never for Phil, for whom Science provided all explanations. Everything was so big, so complex, but I wonder if he ever thought why we were actually here, what was the purpose of being here and what or who actually created the Science? There has to be a reason and there has to be a purpose. Otherwise what is the point? God was the purpose and God was love, God was beauty and goodness. Maybe I didn't have all the answers but I knew what I felt and I was certain that what I felt was right. I knew that the rest of my life would be led by my faith.

Tonight I would tell my work friends - simply to tell them about myself, nothing more. I had resolved that I would tell them all together, tonight.

Debbie

We were all sat eating our desserts when Stella said something about her church. The atmosphere completely and suddenly changed. It was almost like the whole restaurant had gone abruptly eerily quiet and still. The taste of cheesecake and white wine mixed uneasily in my stomach. Kate and Pippa looked incredulous and Lyn started questioning her about it.

I was too busy gauging the effect that two large glasses of wine had also had on me, to think too much of it. I was trying to suppress the overwhelming feeling of nausea that was spreading over me and eventually dashed off to the loo. I managed to throw up quickly and quietly and no-one even looked up, when I made my way back to the table. The atmosphere was still quite serious and Stella seemed to be justifying her churchy stuff. If there is a God, I thought, why does he make me suffer like this?

I could tell the others were very surprised about Stella and I was secretly pleased that one of our group was different - maybe this would keep any attention away from me and my shyness. Any analysis or questioning would relate to why she was religious when she really wasn't at all the type. Surely if anyone wasn't going to fit in as such, it would now have to be her, rather than me. The incredulity of the others was palpable; they obviously thought she was a bit strange. Well maybe - just maybe, I should have more chance of blending in and not being noticed.

However, part of me was also disappointed in her. I could see now that Stella was just being Christian towards me. The lifts she had given me and the friendly comments were all no doubt part of any Christian attitude. One thing I really hated was thinking that anyone pitied me. Did she also pity me somehow or worse still would she think that I was the type that needed to convert?

The conversation was strained for quite a while and I knew the others were trying to get over this small shock. Stella definitely didn't seem the churchy type, but who knows what went on in other people's minds? I know I struggled with the thoughts that chased around my own head, to the extent that I wondered sometimes if I was losing touch with reality. On balance I thought it was good that Stella had let this secret out of the bag, but I made a mental note not to trust her too much and certainly not regard her as a good friend. Her motives now had to be questioned.

Pippa.

I decided to go straight home after a night out with the girls, at the Italian. Normally, I would have tried to persuade them to go clubbing, but I just wasn't in the mood, somehow. To be honest I was a bit taken aback when Stella had started bleating on about church and all that. How annoying and how not cool, I thought, when we were getting on so well. Well, perhaps she was just into it, short term or something?

I didn't know anyone else who was religious and couldn't believe that Stella had seemed so normal up to now! No-one at my previous office was into God, no-one from school or college, none of the girls from Netball or the Gym. I was sure that I had never had any churchy friends because they were just not my type. Stella wasn't the type either, though, it was well strange.

I half wondered about going round to see Nan and I knew this was always my reaction when I was unsettled about anything. Of course it was too late for me to go round though - I knew she would be in bed by now. Also I would never want to worry her. Nan was great; she had brought me up on her own after my Mum had died when I was a toddler. I treasured some pictures I had of Mum, but was sad that I could only remember her kind of vaguely. She was lovely looking and Nan has told me that I take after her in spirit as well as looks. She was so full of life apparently. Never knew my Dad and don't care anyway as he obviously didn't care about me. I'm pretty sure Nan doesn't know who he is either, but as I say, I really don't care.

The flat was quiet and empty when I let myself in, so I put on some loud music and rooted round the kitchen cupboards to find some alcohol. I thought perhaps it wasn't cool to have another drink on my own, but I wanted the numbing feeling to stem the unusual frustration I felt with Stella. We all had such a totally good laugh together and now that all felt a bit ruined by this religious stuff. I wondered about ringing Gary, but decided I wasn't in the mood for him, either. Gary would assume that by coming round here, that we would end up in bed together and I definitely wasn't in the mood for sex. I didn't need him. I guessed we weren't actually that well suited, because we never talked much. Well not, like, really talked.

My thoughts turned to Marcus who had bought this flat and kind of given it to me when we split up. I still was paying a small mortgage which was manageable as Marcus had put down such a huge deposit in the first place. Fair enough that his parents were loaded but he had treated me pretty well all things considered. I knew that his financial generosity might have been down to trying to keep a door open on our relationship but that was not going to happen. I knew he was a decent enough guy, but the whole money and posh background thing got in the way somehow. I never could explain it to him properly but I felt like I was almost another possession and knew that at some time or another he would end up screwing around. It was just a question of time. Dumping him was self-preservation as much as anything, I reckoned.

53

It was a good job I had no cigarettes in the flat. I really fancied a fag even though I had quit smoking over a year ago. I found a half bottle of whisky, a leftover from the Marcus days and poured a good treble into a glass. Topping it up with some diet coke from the fridge, I collapsed on the sofa with my phone to see who I could chat with on Facebook. There was totally no way I would be going to bed in the next hour or so, even if I had work tomorrow. Perhaps work would be more bearable with a hangover!

Debbie.

I suppose I shouldn't have expected it to get any easier at work. Although I knew the answers to most of the questions that the customers asked, I still felt nervous the entire time that I was dealing with them. The worst thing was checking their evidence of looking for work - if they didn't provide this, we were meant to refer them on to an Advisor and warn them that their benefit could be stopped. After three months of signing they were meant to take any job they were capable of doing. So I could be telling some professional type that they should be looking at cleaning or pub jobs!

Pippa really made me feel worse during our tea breaks as she often seemed to recount incidents which made me look pathetic or her look good. The others always laughed at her tales, thereby increasing my shame and humiliation. However, I had to remain here and I had to cope, in order to stay with my friends. I might not say much, but I was part of something - I was part of the group.

There had also been a few religious discussions, following Stella's revelations on the pizza night. Pippa seemed quite put out about it and Lyn had to act as peace maker on a couple of occasions. Well I suppose she likes to extend her boss role a bit outside of work, as well as in. As usual, I wasn't really involved in all the debate but certainly didn't feel any obligation to defend Stella.

Although I was smirking to myself, I think Kate was a bit too sarcastic, though, when she dismissed Stella as being brainwashed. At least Stella or any of the others weren't around when she made the remark though. Perhaps she was sharing her opinion with me because she presumed I wouldn't tell them what she thought. Again and again, I envied Kate. She had all the answers somehow; nothing ever fazed her and she was always laughing.

Anyway, Lyn has invited us all round to her place, for a girly night in. I did accept the offer of a lift from Stella, feeling somehow quite mature for doing so. I am trying so hard to make any socialising seem normal, but of course I am still as anxious as ever.

At home I rarely write in my journal now which I had begun when I started at the job centre. When I read it back now, it all sounds a bit paranoid and obsessive about my friends. Instead I am continually looking through Facebook, reading and re - reading all their various exchanges and occasionally daring to add a comment. I agonise over what to add to my profile and how to word things. I know all the others have loads of photos - Lyn and Stella even have some family shots amongst all of the typical party pictures. I have none.

Lyn.

Rich wasn't too impressed when I said I wanted him out of the way on Saturday night. I just thought he would feel out of place with the girls coming round and I was a bit worried that all the debates about religion might flare up again. I was hoping that after quite a lot of discussion everyone might pipe down and keep their thoughts to themselves. After all what did it really matter what you believed as long as you hurt nobody else and respected others? Each to their own was my philosophy and wherever possible I would avoid any confrontation.

Perhaps I was surrounded by like - minded people as I knew all of my family and Richard's were pretty easy going folk. It was very rare for any of us to really argue over anything although I presumed our views could be quite different. I felt very lucky to be part of such a supportive family and tried never to take this for granted. Rich and I were quite family orientated, choosing to spend time with both sides of our extended families together and always being there for each other. I supposed that was how I also viewed friendships and I hoped that my work friends would stick together.

I had already drunk two glasses of red wine, when the doorbell went. They all arrived at the same time. Stella had driven, so I didn't push her to drink as much as the others. I wondered briefly if she had church friends and wondered what they would think of us. I was surprised that Pippa didn't start up on any religious questions, as she hadn't let up for most of the week, at work. She came out with just a few jibes, which Stella deflected, with equally good humour. I felt relieved that everything was light hearted and easy going. Life was too short to get too serious!

Maybe it was the drink, but I felt the evening went really well. We all got the giggles chatting about other people at work and some of the scenes with the claimants. I even started to think that maybe work would be ok again. So long as you had friends you could have a laugh with, what more could you want? What did it matter if the work was crap?

They didn't end up leaving until about three in the morning, we were all so animated. What did it matter if Stella was a Christian - it just wasn't a problem. Having had coffee around midnight I still felt wide awake and wanted to chat to Rich. However he was fast asleep having gone to bed a few hours back so I didn't think it was fair to wake him.

I mused further about the girls. I knew for sure that I didn't have any issues with Stella and thought that the religious discussions or arguments had probably run their course. I was however somewhat wary of Debbie. Apart from occasional comments and rare odd sarcasm, she seemed to be quieter than ever. It was as though she was retreating into a shell rather than coming out of it. I didn't know anything about her life outside of work and certainly didn't know what she thought or felt. The nagging idea that she didn't like me for some reason somehow played on my mind. I know everyone thought I was really chilled out but actually sometimes I thought I could get quite stressed. Recently the stuff around being a supervisor at work was a lot more difficult as the rules we were meant to enforce got stricter and stricter. Of course dealing with staff was sometimes worse than dealing with the people signing on; you really needed to have some friends or work would just be awful.

Debbie

I was dreading my probation interview with Lyn. It was over three months since I had started working for the job centre and I probably hadn't had one good night's sleep in all that time. It was strange, because on the one hand I was excited to have friends- friends that were outgoing, confident and cool - all the things that I wasn't. On the other hand, I was in a state of constant turmoil; I hated the job and dealing with the public and I worried relentlessly, every time we went out socially.

Even just going round to Lyn's house last week, was a trial. It bugged me to think how easily everything came to Lyn - she was obviously happy with her husband and home and nothing ever seemed to worry her, even at work. Her house was a cottage style terrace – small but bright and very modern inside. What would they ever think of my house - well Mum and Dad's house? It is small and clean obviously, but over fussy and so old fashioned. They are old, of course - in their late fifties, but act more like pensioners in their eighties or nineties!

I knew the others would probably laugh their way through their interviews with Lyn, but I thought I would have to be serious, because I knew she had reservations about me. She had everything going for her, I thought bitterly. I had nothing. It was so unfair that she should have such power over me, but there was nothing I could do about it.

She started off the interview by telling me to relax and that I should just be treating it as a chat. Well that obviously meant that she realised I was nervous. Damn, damn, damn! She proceeded to trot out the same sort of stuff she had done previously with me. She knew I found it a bit stressful dealing with difficult customers, but that was just fine and to be expected and other such platitudes. She kept praising me for the boring aspects of the work - the paperwork, attention to detail - basic skills that didn't require any strength of character. I certainly couldn't imagine her having the same conversation with Stella, Kate or Pippa!

My only comfort was that at least she confirmed that I had passed my probation, but I'm sure that I was still being monitored in some way. I guessed that Lyn would have shared her reservations about me with Pete, which upset me terribly. It was all so easy for her, so smug with nothing to worry about.

Pete was always friendly to me and although I knew a relationship was out of the question, I loved the occasional contact we had - a wry smile or an odd few words, together. When back in my room alone at night, I would daydream and fantasise about Pete. I imagined him asking me out and I had countless imaginary conversations with the others about our relationship and how good we were together. My favourite recurring daydream was me being sympathetic to Pippa who had become jealous of us. If only!

Stella.

God works in mysterious ways....we've had loads of
spiritual debates, but if anything, I think it's made them
think and even question some of their beliefs. I have felt
kind of closer to Lyn and Pippa particularly and I'm not
frightened about talking about the church and my faith.
Most of the time it doesn't feature in our conversations, as
I know that it will take time for them to be fully accepting
of who and what I am.

I guess having gone through the debates and incredulity
from my family, helped me to deal with non - Christian
friends about my faith. This was especially the case when
Phil was home at week-ends because he was the one who
questioned and teased me most about it. When all six of us
were sat around the dining table having our Sunday roast I
felt so much at home, so much a part of the family, that it
was strange to think my spiritual life was something
completely separate.

I have my prayer meetings and the night I help out at the
homeless shelter but I can talk about all this now. It's
great to be honest and open with friends and with my
family. Even though the job isn't maybe what I want to do
long term, I'm pleased to have made such good friends
there. Mum and Dad are keen to discuss my career plans,
but I just want to enjoy where I am for now. It so feels
right. I don't even care too much about buying my own
flat, at the moment. Our wages are poor and I would need
to get another job, in order to get a mortgage. That can
wait, for now, I thought.

Also I did feel that I was able to help the customers more, now I knew what I was doing. It gave me a real buzz when people came back to thank me, for helping them find a job. If only we had more time for each interview, I think I could do even more to help. I can't really think like that though, because there's always a queue and it's not fair to them or the others, if you take too long with one person. Lyn has picked up on the fact that I've been getting some good feedback from the customers - one guy even bought me in a box of chocolates for helping him find a job. Pippa laughed saying she reckoned he just fancied me, but Lyn said that I had done well and although we weren't meant to keep gifts, she could see that he really wanted me to have them. The guy was just so obviously pleased to be signing off. She's very generous with praising us all for our efforts and I continue to learn from her in the way she always goes the extra mile for people. Lyn treats everyone as individuals, which I can see not everyone else does and often that's when trouble can flare up.

The days went by quickly and we always seemed to be laughing whenever we got the chance to get together, at snatched tea breaks and lunch sometimes, at work, or on nights out. It felt good and now that the work was less intimidating, I actually felt quite at home. I even realised that I was doing something useful and that I was pretty good at it! However, occasionally I found my mind sort of wandered and I would be staring out of the window at the clouds floating by. One late afternoon, the sun was sinking slowly, the sky was a painter's dream and I thought, one day I will use my damn Art degree. I wasn't sure how or when but the time would come and it would be right. Something would happen, something would change in my life and I would have more purpose. I wanted and needed to make a difference, somehow.

Debbie

Everyone at work has been talking about Dawn's leaving
do. Apparently the turnover of staff here is huge, which
doesn't surprise me, but Dawn, who is Pete's counterpart,
has been here for ten years, or more, apparently.
Therefore, this was a big deal as Lyn informed us. She
said that it was really unusual for the entire office to be
invited out on a leaving do and that it would be a real
laugh to see what everyone was like outside of work.
Kate, cynical and as outspoken as ever, said she thought
half of them would be too wimpy to go clubbing and Pippa
immediately agreed. How easily I could have fitted in
with the wimps I thought. What was it that had kept me a
part of this group? How on earth was I almost a part of the
cool set?

Sometimes I wondered if I should try and make more
effort to be friendly with other staff - after all there were
many other staff around our age, as well as a lot of older
ones. Perhaps I could be more a part of something else;
maybe I wouldn't feel so intimidated and nervous. The
awful sense of foreboding that had begun way back when I
had started this job, had never left me. I felt like I was
continually fighting specific imminent anxieties and
somewhat vague future worries. My insecurity knew no
bounds.

Dawn was leaving because she had applied for a job in the
Regional Office, which was a promotion, apparently. I
wondered if Pete had also gone for this post, as he was the
same grade. I also considered if he would be going to the

leaving do and decided that it was very likely. What should I wear? Should I drink that night? Would I have the courage to talk to him?

Kate.

How boring all that religious crap from Stella, dominating
all our conversations, lately. Anyhow, things might be
looking up at last! The whole office has been invited to
Dawn's leaving do. I'm sure Pete will be there and no
doubt Pippa will try and get off with him. Maybe I could
put a spanner in the works, if I could be bothered. Pete
wasn't really that fit and I reckoned that Pippa may only be
after him to try and get her promotion. Stupid cow, she's
so shallow.

Although I thought some of the office staff probably
wouldn't even go on the night out, it would be interesting
to see whoever turned up. "Shades" where we've been
before was a bit chavvy, typical for Pippa's taste, but
pathetic Debbie appeared scared, the entire time we were
there. I guessed she would be even more petrified by
going on to "The Academy" - the biggest, coolest club in
town and the venue Dawn has chosen for the night out!

I wondered what Stella would be like - she had seemed so
totally cool before she came out with her I'm a Christian
stuff. Lyn was doing her usual cop out of sitting on the
fence, with saying stuff like "each to their own" but I
thought it was best not to join in, too much. Pippa wasn't
slow in voicing her opinions, which seemed the complete
opposite of Stella's - but even she wasn't as dismissive as I
felt. I reckoned only people with problems turned to God
so I thought maybe that Debbie would want to go along
with Stella's church, but perversely she stayed as quiet as
ever.

What rubbish, it all was. We're all animals, how can there be some cosy Heaven, to look forward to? How can people kid themselves so easily? Weird about Debbie though as she seems the churchy type - but strangely she was with the rest of us, on this. Safety in numbers, no doubt…not that she like, joins in with stuff hardly at all.

I tried to get her to open up a bit by telling her that Stella was just brainwashed by the whole religious thing, but I didn't even get a response. So, Stella will be on her own, flying the God flag. Actually after a week or so the arguments died and not much has been said since, so let's hope it doesn't come up on Dawn's night out. Let's hope everyone has better things to do - like getting completely wasted!

Debbie.

My nervousness had increased the nearer it got to Dawn's do and now tonight was the night. I seriously thought I had something major wrong with me - my heart was pounding faster than ever before, my nausea was overwhelming and I somehow felt disjointed from the sights and sounds that surrounded me. Stella and I had just arrived in the club.

I had insisted that it was my turn to drive, which of course meant I had an excuse to turn down any alcoholic drinks. I gathered that others found alcohol relaxing, but it was too much of a risk for me. What little control I retained, emotionally or even physically, could be compromised by the unknown effect that the drinks may have on me. Who knows - perhaps I could be really ill, not just nervous! I was too young to be having a heart attack, surely? Maybe I had contracted some fatal mystery virus that was quickly ravaging my body? Did I care if I was dying? Well, "living ain't easy", as some pop song said.
I tried to calm myself down, thinking about a few recent conversations people had had about Dawn. Although she was about Lyn's age or a bit older, she was very slim and attractive. However there were rumours that she had suffered with anorexia since her late teens and that she still forced herself to throw up after big meals. She hadn't wanted to go out for a meal for her leaving do, therefore. Apparently another much younger girl in the office was also meant to have an eating disorder, so I knew the whole anxiety thing was experienced by others. Their worry only related to food though, which I guess related to how they looked, but it was crazy because they both looked so good.

No my anxiety was worse, it was all encompassing - it was ruining my entire life.

I was so consumed with my paranoiac thoughts, that I hadn't realised a group from the office had joined us. Lyn asked if I was ok, almost straight away. Oh why did she have to draw attention to me?
"Let's grab that free table" Kate announced.
Stella proceeded to take everyone's drinks orders and wandered off to the bar, linking arms with Pippa.
"You've got some catching up to do babe!" Pippa said.

"Right" Lyn shouted above the loud music "who here hasn't met Rich?"
As the introductions were being made, I looked surreptitiously around the table. About a dozen of us or more altogether and no-one was looking remotely nervous. I felt quite sweaty and worried that my underarm deodorant would prove ineffective, as it had on a few other occasions. Keep smiling and try to follow the conversations, I thought. Think now about how you can get through this evening without dancing. Of course, this was another potential source of humiliation. Why was I even here - I didn't belong here.

Pippa and Stella came back, giggling, with trays loaded with Vodka Redbulls.
"It's still Happy Hour" Stella smiled "Two for the price of one!"
"Drink up, then" replied Lyn "Let's get another round in."
I tried really hard to join in, to be a part of the banter, but it was so difficult to focus on anything other than my nerves and all the completely real physical ailments that

accompanied this. My immediate aim was not to give in to the waves of nausea that were passing over me. I had to control myself, deep breaths, engage in what was going on around me and think "you're in with the in crowd" or other such similar self - deceptive motivations.

Imagine my horror, then when a few guys approached our side of the table and asked some of us to dance.
"Why not?" I heard Kate say and felt my body get up and head towards the dance floor. I couldn't see or hear anything, but allowed myself to be led by one spotty individual, who for whatever reason had singled me out. Would he know that I couldn't dance? I had to concentrate on keeping my arms by my sides - I could now feel the damp patches spreading under my arms. I was bumped and jostled as we made our way on to the dance floor. At least the music was so loud that it precluded conversation and the incessant flashing lights made it impossible to look at anyone too closely.

The youth opposite me was swaying and clicking his fingers a bit, but didn't seem that confident about dancing. He wasn't much taller than me and his lank longish hair covered a good part of his spotty face. How ironic, I thought that I was almost feeling sorry for someone else and I assumed that he would hate to think he was being pitied, just as much as I did.
How I also wished that I could maintain these odd moments of clarity and rational thought.

71

Pippa

Looking over at the dance floor, I couldn't help but feel a bit sorry for poor old Debbie.

"Look" I remarked to Lyn. "Debbie looks petrified - she's so totally stiff. Do you think she's ever had a boyfriend?"

"Doubt it" Lyn returned "and where's yours tonight, may I ask?"

I explained to her about Gary. He was ok, but we weren't serious and I felt like keeping my options open tonight. Good job too, as Pete had just arrived. Before he had a chance to sit down, I grabbed hold of him and steered him over to the dance floor. On our way over, an extremely flustered looking Debbie hurried past us. I saw Stella dancing with some bloke, so went over and asked her what was going on.

"Dunno. She just said she was going to the loo - maybe she was trying to get away from him."

I followed Stella's eyes over to some young lad, on his own, swaying slightly and looking a bit embarrassed.

Pete wasn't a bad dancer and his clothes were quite cool - a much better impression than he gave at work! I knew that a lot of staff would be here from the office and I guessed that I would be the main topic of conversation, right now. I didn't care what anyone thought - it wasn't as though he was married or anything. So what if he was a Manager at work - He wasn't my immediate boss and I'm sure he wasn't that much older than me.

After a few dances, we spent most of the evening together and it surprised me how well we got on. He was a totally

good laugh and we seemed to just click somehow. So
much so, that I decided to invite him back to mine for
coffee. I was secretly pleased when Lyn acknowledged
what was going on.

"If you like him, go for it! He's a good bloke. Straight
up." She said.

Back at my flat, we carried on chatting into the early
hours. It was great actually to just, like, talk. Despite
myself, I was impressed that he made no move on me, but
we shared a deliciously long snog, on the doorstep, as he
left. We had agreed to meet the next day - Sunday
afternoon - wanting to see each other again, before we
were back at work. I was pretty sure Pete normally played
five a side football on Sunday afternoons, but kept my
mouth firmly shut.

Debbie.

The day after Dawn's leaving do, I sat in my room, trying to assess the evening. Complete disaster, I thought. Never again, was my over-riding summary. Perhaps, I should have been flattered that I had been asked to dance, but it just opened me up to ridicule. The final straw had been seeing Pippa, commandeering poor Pete. I had managed to regain some composure in the loos, but had made excuses for myself, by reporting back to the others that I thought I was going down with some bug. It occurred to me that I could continue this excuse to avoid going to work tomorrow - it would be easy enough to fool Mum and Dad, too. Not that they would care as all they ever do is watch TV. Well Mum cooks and cleans and Dad mutters opinions at the TV. They never talk to me and not much at all to each other.

Kate had initially seemed incensed about Pippa and Pete, but then went into her superior, dismissive mode, suggesting to me that Pippa was out for promotion and that Pete must be hard up. Once again, I envied her self-confidence and resolute outlook on life - we were just complete opposites. Actually I thought that Kate may be a bit jealous - I knew I was, but then I also knew that I would never ever have any chance with someone like Pete.

Lyn and Stella were both typically pragmatic - although I never knew with either of them if they ever really opened up with me. They had seemed concerned when I had said that I felt unwell - or was their concern just pity - was I so pathetic, that all I invoked was pity? They had both been chatting about Dawn, saying how sad it was about her anorexia and had come up with various theories as to how such things start up. Social pressures, media images, trying to avoid adulthood, attention seeking and even insecure childhoods, had been discussed.

"Still this is way too serious a conversation to be having in a nightclub" Lyn had said and had turned in the other direction to chat with Richard. So then, Stella had looked round to me and asked
"What do you think then Debbie? Why do so many girls have eating disorders?"
I had tried to look dismissive like Kate often was.
"Lyn's right - this is way too serious a subject to talk about whilst we're in a club!"

Luckily, she hadn't chosen to pursue it any further. I was thinking that it was dangerous territory, that the conversation could have led to chat about stress in general, people not coping in general, or worst of all, questions about me, specifically about me. When Stella had then started to chat about some of our other work colleagues that were in the club, I had pretended I had difficulty in hearing. That was fair enough, the music had been ridiculously loud. I remembered that I had glanced surreptitiously at my watch, wondering how much longer we had been expected to stay.

"If you're not feeling too well, don't worry about giving me a lift" Stella had shouted. She was bound to have seen the relief that had surely flooded my face.
"Ok if you're sure" I had replied.

I had made a few quick cursory goodbyes and taken a last look over to the dance floor, before making my exit. Pippa was slow dancing with Pete, her arms were firmly around his neck and she was smiling up into his face without a care or fear in the world. I felt like I had just been stabbed with a knife straight into my heart.

Lyn.

Typical Monday morning with two people phoning in sick and I could have predicted one of them would be Debbie. She had sounded a bit apologetic but more vague and scared than anything else, saying the bug she had started on Saturday had got worse. I made a quick phone call to Pete to see if it would be worth trying to get some help from the other Sections, but he said they were all short staffed too. I guessed I would end up helping out with the signing at some point so that we wouldn't end up with people waiting for too long, getting stroppy.

As there were less people around I had to be more careful with staff rotas for break times and suggested to Pippa that we could both change our usual times to go on an early lunch to make sure there was adequate cover.
"Besides which" I said to her "I want to hear all about you and Pete!"
A huge smile covered her face which she half tried to cover with her hand.
"Yeah ok babe - but let's go out and grab a coffee, I don't want half the tea room listening in on us."
A few hours later we were sat in Luigi's both nursing large mugs of steaming cappuccinos. Although the coffee was really hot I was taking small sips, anxious to get the caffeine hit and the feeling of reward after a busy and stressful morning of a constant queue of people waiting to sign on and some of them then ranting at the staff for enduring the delay. I looked at my watch and thought with relief that we could at least have half an hour or so respite, before we would have to head back to the office.

"He's actually real cute. Nothing went on - well not like you're probably thinking." Pippa said in a rush.

"I'm not thinking anything." I smiled. "I wouldn't have put you two together though - Pete's pretty quiet - so I'm just curious how you got along generally."

"Yeah I thought he was, like, shy, but when there's just the two of us, we are both talking non-stop. When he came back for coffee, we ended up chatting until about four in the morning. Then on Sunday afternoon, we met in town and the time just totally flew by. He takes me seriously, you know?" she said.

"Wow. Is this the Pippa we've all come to know and love? It almost seems as though you like him because he's a nice guy then?" I asked.

Pippa laughed. "Oh my God, no, but he's fit and all. I'm guessing I will be the gossip of the tea room today? "

"Too right. We've played into their hands by coming out now, you do realise? Still it stops them bitching about someone else and the speculation about Dawn's anorexia should pipe down now that she's moved on to Regional Office."

Pippa drained her cappuccino and leant back in her chair. "I've heard that Jess is being promoted to take Dawn's post. Why didn't you go for that? You could have been a Manager alongside Pete." she said.

"Bit early days for me and way too much responsibility, I reckon. No I'm happy being a Supervisor for now." I replied.

"Well they will need someone in Jess's old job now, so I may go for that." Pippa said whilst looking intently at me.

"Go for it." I said.

"I mean it, definitely." I added as her face registered unusual anxiety and reticence.

The time soon went and we were going back to the Office. I reflected on what Pippa had been saying. Maybe I should have been going for the next grade. Maybe being a Higher Executive Officer could turn out to be less stressful than being just an Executive Officer. As an Executive Officer you were either a Supervisor of a Section or a specialist Advisor and neither role was easy. Would it be better just to get out completely though, I wondered.

Debbie.

Sitting alone at home, I replayed the scenes of Saturday night over and over in my head. I couldn't rid myself of the image of Pippa looking so smug dancing with Pete. Why couldn't I have stayed with the poor bloke who I had been dancing with? Running off like that had made me look stupid and no doubt everyone at work was talking about it now. Stella had then provided me with an excuse of leaving early if I felt unwell but little did she know that I was often in such turmoil. I half regretted phoning in sick though, as it had only put off the inevitable questions and increased my anticipated fear of humiliation.

Mum didn't question me about being at home on a work day again, but I caught the familiar look of disappointment in her weary tired eyes. Mum never actually comes in my room but knocks apologetically at the door calling me to join them for tea. Dad doesn't even get that near. The three of us then sit quietly around the dining table, with Dad making occasional half- hearted attempts at conversations and Mum responding timidly. Apart from the morose and stifling atmosphere, I never really enjoy the food that Mum prepares. Dull and stodgy, I force it down with surreptitious gulps of water and remind myself to stack the dishwasher afterwards so Dad won't be able to complain about me.

As soon as I can, I head back to the refuge of my room. I cannot resist the temptation to check Facebook immediately. There are a few photos from Dawn's leaving do, but mercifully I do not feature in any of them. Stella had also posted some family pictures which were taken on Sunday lunchtime in a pub. How it contrasted with my family, with her three siblings and young- looking parents: all smiling. They were out for a family lunch as Phil the elder brother was home this week end apparently. Lucky Stella, with one big happy family, I thought enviously.

As I scrolled down something jumped out at me. No! Pete had changed his relationship status from "single" to "in a relationship with Pippa Harris." So he had actually updated his status but she hadn't. It hurt me so much to see how she could be so cool and he was so obviously smitten.

Kate.

God it was old news already but Pippa and Pete were still the gossip of the tea room. Friday lunchtime was usually the time that most of us had a cheap meal in the local but I was a bit bored with that scene and got Debbie to come with me to Luigi's instead. Shit, why follow the crowd anyway? Debbie seemed her usual anxious self, fidgeting and taking periodic miniscule bites from a chocolate brownie.

"What do you think about Pete and Pippa then" she asked, finally.
"It won't last." I retorted. "She's just an empty headed slag and he'll soon get bored with her."
I knew Debbie was quite shocked by what I had said, as she had this weird idea that we were all the best of friends. When was she going to wake up?
Secretly though, I was a bit miffed. He was ok really, was Pete. He should've seen right through Pippa and then maybe we might have become an item, instead of them. I got the idea that Debbie might even fancy him too, but God she had no hope. Pete wasn't even that fit, but he was well out of Debbie's league!

I kind of forgot that Debbie was with me and was dreamily fantasising about Pete dumping Pippa to go out with me. I reckoned if I really put my mind to it that I could make it happen. That would give the whole office something to talk about! Gradually I became aware of Debbie clearing her throat.

"What do you think they're all talking about now?" was her next question.

"How the hell do I know?" I said. "I don't care."

I was actually thinking well if you're that bothered then you should have gone to the damn pub with them in the first place.

When we got back to the office everything seemed really quiet then about a dozen people all piled in doing a conga around the desks. I supposed some of them were a bit wasted from being in the pub but they were all having a right giggle and I immediately regretted going to Luigi's instead of the pub. Bad choice! Debbie though looked a bit reproving, even though there were no Jobseekers nearby and I saw Lyn glance over at her before telling the rest of the group reluctantly that

"That's enough now. We'd better get back to work." Although they stopped dancing and gradually sat down, they all carried on humming the tune of the conga, interspersed with hands slapping on desks. You just had to laugh.

Debbie.

I should listen to Kate; at least she wants to be with me. I know everyone automatically goes off to the pub, without fail; every Friday lunchtime, but no-one had specifically said anything to me about it this week. I had the impression that some of the other staff on our Section did not like the fact that I had been off sick on Monday and Tuesday, as Lyn and Stella were the only two that had asked if I was feeling better. So I was surprised and pleased that Kate suggested going to Luigi's instead of the pub.

I would love to have the carefree dismissive attitude that Kate has. Even though I suspected she was a bit jealous of Pippa for having ensnared Pete, I think she almost saw the situation as a challenge and was probably plotting on breaking them up. It amazes me that someone as brash as Kate shows any interest at all in mousy old me. I'm sure she says what she likes to me, though, because she knows I wouldn't remonstrate with her, or more importantly, tell the others what she thinks of them. Perhaps I am just a sounding board for her so she can be quite bitchy.

When we had returned to the office, the rare peace was shattered when they all came back from the pub. I felt so apart from everyone as they appeared to be having such fun, but I really didn't understand why they were all laughing so much.

Stella.

Pete and one of his mates Johny had started sitting with our gang, every so often, in the tea room and Johny had a great sense of humour as well as being cute.
Problem was that he was gay, so there was no chance of anything happening. I realised that some people in our church were a bit sort of anti- gay, but I couldn't see that God would be that judgemental. It was a shame though and I wondered once again, actually if it would be possible for me to have a relationship with a non- Christian, anyway. I thought not.

Johny was the centre of attention as usual, doing a perfect impression of the big boss, Jerry.
"Could we have a little less chat and a little bit more work, people?" He mimicked. He then continued to talk about how he felt Friday lunch times in the local pub were the only good part of the working week.
"Johny, I don't know how you manage to work in the afternoon after three or four beers." Pete laughed.
Johny then turned to me and asked "Why wasn't your mate Debbie in the pub today? I think I saw her, on her own, in Luigi's."
"We're not joined at the hip" I answered defensively.
"Can't say I missed her," Pippa added. "She's a bit well weird sometimes don't you think?"
Everyone laughed but then I felt terrible as I looked up and saw Debbie in the kitchen staring over at us. She must have been coming in for a break and overheard the conversation, because she turned straight around and ran back out.

"Pippa, Debbie was in the kitchen and I think she may have heard you." I said.

"Oh my God. Totally not cool, do you think I should say anything to her or like, apologise or what?" Pippa looked pretty upset.

"I would just leave it." Johny said. "She will get over it. You can't take it back and it wasn't like you were being really bitchy or anything."

I thought Johnny's advice was sound, but even so I had a bad feeling in my stomach. Debbie's face seemed full of anguish, I would have to try and make it up to her somehow. She was such a little lost soul who struggled to cope.

Debbie.

I couldn't believe what I had just heard, Pippa saying I was
weird! The worst thing about it though was everyone else
laughing in response. Where could I go? What could I do?
I ran to the ladies loos and locked myself quickly in a
cubicle. At least Johny had wondered why I hadn't been
in the pub; he must have gone by Luigi's when Kate was
up at the counter ordering our coffees and cakes. Even
Stella was being mean about me but at least Kate and Lyn
weren't there at the time. I had to pull myself together and
head back to my desk - I couldn't stay here hidden away
for much longer, no matter how much I wanted to.

Walking down the corridor, it was typical that I passed
Lyn striding off in the opposite direction.
 "All right, Debbie?" she asked.
"Yes, why shouldn't I be?" I countered and hurried on by,
my eyes averted.
I hadn't actually been crying, but I supposed it may look as
if I had.

Pippa.

Stella seemed a bit freaked out that Debbie had heard me slagging her off, but I wasn't going to lose sleep over it. It wasn't like we were real good mates or anything, but I guess I did feel a bit bad about it. I had had more than my fair share of stuff worse than that. Girls who I had thought were my friends bitched about me over the years, but that was just jealousy. Oh my God, she should just get over it - it's not like I could say anything to make up for it anyway.

I sensed that a few of the staff were totally against me going out with Pete, but that was their problem. Jealousy, again. I well liked the fact that we were the main topic of gossip at work and even texted Pete to meet me in the stationary store room, planning on a quick sneaky snog. If we got caught out, so much the better! It was still talked about that a couple having an affair had been caught having sex in there during a Christmas Party a few years back and I wondered if Pete would remember that. Tacky, but funny.

My timing was crap though. Jerry of all people was there at the time I had suggested and Pete smiled ruefully at me as he picked up a box of photo copying paper and went straight back out.

"How's everything going then young lady?" Jerry asked me. I realised immediately that he didn't even know my name and was looking straight at my cleavage. We were the only two people here, now.

"Fine." I replied, whilst thinking what a wanker! I could tell he wanted to keep me talking but he couldn't think of anything to say and it made me smile. He may be the big boss but he was also just a dirty old man with no guts. He stood there; not knowing what to say or what to do.

I picked up some envelopes and sauntered out. Another time, I thought as I looked at my phone. Pete had just texted one word "Sorry" followed by a few kisses.

Debbie.

I couldn't face going in to work knowing now that I was a laughing stock. Overhearing Pippa had just confirmed my worst fears. How had I once thought we would all be friends? How had I ever imagined I would be part of a group? How had I dared to dream that I could be cool?

I bet Kate never felt nervous; she had all the confidence which I would never have, the bravado, the humour and the not giving a damn attitude. Stella had her God and her family and a sense of calm. Lyn and Pippa were the typical sort of women who had it all. What upset me most was that on top of everything else, Pippa now had Pete. Life was so unfair.

Lyn.

About four months had gone by since Pete and Pippa had first got together and it was no longer a source of such gossip at work. I was surprised, then, when he asked me what people thought, when we were sat in his room, carrying out some staff reviews. I had joked that it might not have gone down too well if she got a really good report.
"But that's just it!" he had retorted. "She is damn good at her job and she has exceeded all her objectives, but people will think I'm just being biased."
I reminded him gently, that it was my decision to recommend the grading and he was only counter signing this. I presumed some staff may possibly be annoyed with me too - the immediate boss and friend, rather than the higher up boss and now lover.

My concern was not Pippa, though, or her relationship, come to that; it was how to proceed with Debbie. Debbie had taken a load of time off sick, during the last few months. Most of these had been single days – mostly with general declarations on her self-certification notes, such as migraine, cold, cough, or virus. At this stage, I was meant to be giving a verbal warning and if she took any more time off in the next three months, then she could be on a written warning. Pete asked me the usual questions around if I thought there was an underlying problem and if it was stress related.

Pete reminded me that I would have to give Debbie the opportunity to bring someone with her to our interview.

91

The Union guy was a bit of a dope-head, but I thought it might go better with him there. At least I wouldn't be on my own with her again. I knew I should try to get her to admit to being stressed out and then we could perhaps help her out more. I also needed to try and get her to talk to the Counselling Service.

In all the years I had been in the job, many staff had taken early retirement on medical grounds and loads more had left to take up other less stressful jobs. Pete and I agreed that Debbie was probably stressed out, but neither of us knew how to resolve this. Of course we knew all the right management techniques of encouragement, team work, training and minimising disruption through planning and prioritising tasks. What we couldn't do was supply the right number of staff to cope with the volume of work. We were always being told that cut backs were necessary, but half the time the new recruits were less than the corresponding numbers who had left. At the moment, when we knew unemployment was going up, we actually had a recruitment freeze, which was crazy when staff were still leaving in their droves. It was worse than it had ever been.

Some people though, just weren't right for dealing with the public - they didn't cope with certain situations at all. I felt Debbie wasn't helping herself or maybe she just didn't know how? She gave so little information about herself; but surprised me sometimes with a rare sarcastic or almost aggressive comment. There had to be a reason why she was so withdrawn and defensive. I felt that she must have other problems outside work, but couldn't get her to open up. I was also convinced now that she disliked me; but felt this was unfair and unreasonable.

The other big problem was the effect of staff going off sick. By now every morning on my way into work, I was performing varying estimates of who would be phoning in sick, that day. Pete volunteered to sit in with me for Debbie's next monitoring interview but I declined, thinking it would stress her out, even more than usual.

Next week was going to be particularly bad for staff cover, as there was to be a planned strike on Thursday. I felt in all conscience that I should go out with the strikers, as I agreed with all the grievances - having to work for much longer for a reduced amount of pension and salary freezes which were actually more like pay cuts when taking inflation into consideration. Rich reckoned a lot of his mates weren't too happy about proposed cuts for the Police, too and we both wondered where it would all end.

I gathered that about half the staff would probably not be showing up for work on Thursday and that made me feel guilty about the ones who did turn up and the extra work that would be expected from them. Oh well, I knew it was up to Jerry, or even a directive from Regional Office, to simply shut the place down for a day, cancel any signing on and then at least there wouldn't be all the usual problems with the public. Again I wondered really why I was still in this job; maybe it was because I had made good friends in the past and we had had such a laugh at the start? There was still that same sense of pulling together in pretty adverse circumstances and seeing humour in all things, but perhaps now I needed to make a concerted effort to look for something else.

Of course the timing was bad now - what with lots of cut backs, redundancies and some firms going under. Perhaps I should be grateful that I had this job - that I had any job. That was the philosophy that kept the workers in line; I thought - kept us doing more hours and taking on more responsibility than we were paid for and kept us in jobs that stressed everyone out. It was definitely time to move on - if ever I was able to.

Debbie.

I knew it would come to this. A façade of concern and politeness, but Lyn was informing me that I was on a warning, because of the time I had taken off sick. I couldn't bear the thought of someone else witnessing my discomfort, so I had turned down the offer of having the Union chap Dave or anyone else sitting in with me. Dave was rumoured to be some sort of drug addict, although Pippa had laughingly dismissed this saying that
"He only smoked pot once in a while."
Well I didn't think Dave, or anybody else for that matter, would be able to help me.

How could Lyn begin to imagine the struggle I went through, just to come to work in the morning! She kept asking me if I was stressed, but I wasn't going to admit to that. Why couldn't she just leave me alone and accept that I was genuinely unwell?

On some of the days I had taken off, I had actually been physically sick - so much so that even Mum had hinted vaguely that I should see a Doctor.
The ignominy of sharing a bathroom with Mum and Dad must have been how Mum had realised I was throwing up on a regular basis. Obviously I didn't clean up to her high standards. She even had a stupid doll-like thing to cover up the loo rolls as if anyone ever saw them! Air fresheners everywhere too, which had the effect of making the whole house smell funny. Mum was always dusting the hoard of cheap little ornaments everywhere. She seemed obsessed with doing all these ridiculous little things, which maybe

she mistook for creating a home. Never any conversation or laughter though - perish the thought.

The interview with Lyn was punctuated with the usual routine silences, which I no longer made any attempt to fill. She bleated on about wanting to help, about other people that could help - some counselling service or other and how she wished I could "be more open" or such like. Well I wasn't going to make her job any easier for her, I thought. Sit tight. Make her - the bitch - keep talking.

She asked me if I was going out on Strike, which was in a couple of days. An opportunity for a day off I immediately thought and mumbled "probably". Lyn wasn't to know that I couldn't really care less about the money we got paid or our pension entitlements. Pensions - that was so far off, when I struggled to see beyond the week or day or even hour we were in. Often at work now, I was almost willing the time to go by when I had to deal with customers, but the clock ticked oh so slowly. Yes a day off without having to phone in sick - of course I would be going on strike!

I couldn't believe now that I had been so optimistic when I started this job. After Pippa and Pete started going out, our group didn't socialise as much. Often I pleaded migraines to avoid these social occasions, in any case. I knew that some of them had played tennis after work a few times, but I hadn't even been invited - not that I could play anyway, of course. I think I overheard Pippa asking Stella and Lyn if they wanted to join some Pub Quiz Team too. I'm pretty sure she deliberately excludes me from many conversations and on other occasions even forgets that I'm there. The only time I might be included by her is when she's laughing at me or belittling me in some way. She had so many friends and so much going on, why should she be bothered with me and why should she have Pete as well. It made my stomach turn to think of Pippa with Pete, poor Pete. Of course it was even worse to listen to her describing their nights out, with that self -satisfied look on her face.

Also at work now I tried to avoid going on a break at the same time as them, preferring to go very early or very late when not many people were in the tea room. It was a relief to just sit on my own and pretend to read one of the dated scruffy and torn magazines left in there. Everything I read about in magazines confirmed to me that I was an utter loser, so why would anyone want to be friends with me?

On the odd occasion when I was sat with them, Lyn was more distant with me and Stella seemed to talk more about her friends from church. Strangely enough I felt that I shared more with Kate, of late, even though I assumed she still regarded me with derision. She called a spade a spade and I admired her for that and envied her total self-confidence which amounted to arrogance - in the job and, well, in all things. At least I could talk to her a bit though, without clamming up or making a complete fool of myself. So much so, that I got enough courage to suggest she would be welcome to call round and see me at home, if she wanted.

Kate.

What the hell, Debbie had got more and more neurotic. She was always comparing herself to the others and falling well short. Whining on about how she wished she could be more confident and popular. Whinging how she was worried that no-one liked her. I had actually decided to pop in on her at her house and virtually immediately regretted my decision. At least her parents were out, so I didn't have to make stupid polite conversation, but Debbie was as nervous as ever. The house looked a bit twee and her bedroom looked like it belonged to a kid, with dated posters stuck on the walls and old fashioned furniture.

She even got to talking about how her parents weren't interested in her; that was completely weird. I thought of it the other way round - I wasn't that bothered what my Mum and Dad thought; they were just there and it suited me to be living at home right now. I told her how good it was that I didn't have to pay my parents much money, so I could save up enough to move out pretty soon. Actually, though, I got on pretty ok with them, but just didn't spend as much time with them as they would probably have liked. Debbie seemed relieved that her Mum and Dad were out - presumably so she didn't have to introduce me! She also really went on and on about Lyn, Stella and Pippa, though. She never, ever, stopped talking about them, which was really obsessive.

"Why should you care what they think?" I admonished her.

I tried to reason with her - couldn't she see that Pippa was an attention seeking tart, Stella was a happy clappy nut and Lyn was smug and self-obsessed.   She probably thought I was being a right old bitch, but I figured everyone was out for themselves and I wasn't one for pussy footing about peoples' feelings. Like, why would they be spending time or wasting time talking about her?

Regardless of what I said, I doubted that Debbie would ever pull herself together; she was way too screwed up. Chances were she wouldn't be in a job much longer either. Lyn was probably out to get rid of her and prove how hard she was. Must be said, though, that Debbie was mad to have skived off sick so much - didn't she know how to play the system?   Stupid, poor kid - she was probably heading for some kind of nervous breakdown!

I did confide in her about what I really thought about Pippa, though. Pippa had continued to get on my nerves. She was so full of herself, so full of shit about her and Pete. I had really started to think she was deluded. Did she imagine anyone was interested in her little charade? I told Debbie that Stella was well gullible enough to be taken in, but surely that Lyn was a bit more street-wise?   I knew that the one of the other supervisors at Lyn's level had been promoted as the replacement for Dawn and soon they would be looking for another Supervisor. Of course Pippa sleeping with Pete made her a prime candidate! How convenient! Everyone must see what she's like, the slag who only ever thinks of herself. She's so fucking obvious and so superficial. Debbie didn't say anything but I reckoned she agreed with everything I had said.

Debbie.

At least I think Kate and I might become friends; she must like me, otherwise she wouldn't have come round to my house, the other day. We are so different but maybe I can learn from her; learn how to be thick- skinned, how to laugh at things and how to be cool. I didn't want to be bitchy like her, though. She thinks a lot of people are saying that Pippa is only with Pete in order to get promoted. I'm sure things can't happen like that, no matter what Kate says. However I do feel sorry for Pete if he is being used. I would be so happy, out of this world happy, just to be his girlfriend that I would never want for anything more. Of course he would never ever view me like that, though, and I suspected that he was becoming quite besotted with Pippa.

Regardless of Kate's visit, I still cannot rid myself of an overwhelming sense of doom. My feelings of foreboding seem to grow; I don't know what I am frightened about, but I just know that something very bad is going to happen.

Stella.

It was quite strange I thought that Lyn had come out on strike with the rest of us. Getting to know her better, I realised she so had a strong social conscience and had a similar political outlook to me. It had surprised me further that Pippa had decided not to strike though - saying she thought it was unfair to leave so few staff in the office, when it had been decided to still be open to the public. Of course Pete may have influenced her as he was going to be in the office that day. On the one hand I was kind of disappointed with her for not showing solidarity with the Action, but on the other hand I couldn't help but admire her for her work commitment. This so didn't go with her party girl image! Also I was pretty sure that many staff had just seen the Strike as an excuse for a day off.

The more I thought about it, the more it made sense. I decided to invite just Lyn and Pippa to our next church meeting. Something had particularly drawn me to these two individuals and I had to provide them with an opportunity to let Jesus into their lives. Not that it would happen probably, but maybe it was worth a go? I appreciated that it wasn't considered cool to bang on about Christianity too much, but after that first week or so of incredulity, argument and debate, nothing much had been said. Obviously, I had prayed for guidance and had decided, for a while at least, not to talk too much about my spiritual life. However, a lot of time had passed now and I sort of felt the time was right. Our friendship had flourished and I so wanted to see if there was any chance they could share the beauty of faith.

I couldn't conceal my pleasure or surprise, when they both agreed to come, albeit with some cynical comments.
"You should keep an open mind," I told them.
I knew I had no individual influence over other people's faith, but at least I was kind of providing an opportunity. The rest was in God's hands.

Part of me wondered if I should've tried to get Debbie to come along, as well. She obviously had a lot of problems and seemed to deliberately avoid spending any time with the rest of us. I hardly ever saw her in the tea room now, particularly after she had overheard Pippa calling her "weird". However, she had shown no interest at all - at least the others questioned and argued. Debbie just seemed so stressed all the time, I supposed because of the job, but it was such sort of hard work to even hold a conversation with her. In fact, days went by now when our paths didn't cross at all.

I didn't envy Lyn - having to be her Supervisor. I guessed it was also pretty hard for her also to be friends with people that she was meant to be in charge of. Not that Debbie was like a friend really. I reckoned Lyn was really cool though by listening to and encouraging everyone and by always mucking in herself. She definitely played a big part in our section having the best team spirit in the office and I was dead chuffed to be a part of it. It was a bit strange that she was ten years older than me, but we seemed to be on the same wavelength and definitely shared the same sense of humour.

I had chatted to Lyn about helping out in the homeless shelter and was pleased that she admired what I was doing and wondered if she would look at trying out some voluntary role for herself. I also said I was looking at trying to get involved with more youth type charity work. Although I felt quite kind of at home now in the job centre, I still felt that I should look to do something more worthwhile in the future and with that in mind, I had started looking at various options. I thought I could try different things out maybe just doing a few hours one evening a week or over the week-end. My first trial had been set up with a youth club through church for next week.

I was a bit nervous about it - after all the kids going there were not a lot younger than me. On the other hand, I supposed that even the older 16 year olds would probably view anyone in their twenties as pretty ancient, so it would definitely be a challenge to try and get on with them. I needed to make a difference and the whole job centre thing wasn't enough for me.

Debbie.

Although I keep trying to take on board what Kate has said about Stella, it still upset me that she only invited Lyn and Pippa to her church. I wish I could be like Kate and just not care about things like this, but I keep thinking what hope I had, for a group of friends, when we had first all met. I am beginning to feel invisible again, just like it was through those long, lonely years at school.

Of course, I have no interest in church or God - it was an easy way out to think that somehow everything was going to be all right in the end. What got to me was the pity I perceived in Stella's eyes. How galling that the so called Christian actually had no real feelings of friendship for me and how much worse that Pippa and Lyn cared enough about her, to pander to her request! How come three wasn't a crowd in this? I knew neither of them was likely to convert or anything so why were they going? I couldn't understand if they were being nice and sympathetic, cold and ironic or just plain curious.

The only thing that makes me go to work now, is the thought of seeing Pete. I'm sure that Pippa can't be really serious about him and he definitely seems to be stopping by my desk, more, to have a chat. He often asks me how I am and on a couple of occasions after I've been off sick, he's said that it was good to see me back. I just think and hope that he genuinely cares and isn't going through the motions, like Lyn. Several weeks had gone by since my first so called warning and I had been called in to see Lyn again, when she produced something in writing. So I was on a six month trial; if I kept having more time off sick, they would sack me - well, eventually.

I'm sure my mouth was formed into a twisted smile as I read through the formal document. What Lyn didn't realise, was that this may be a way out for me! I had never put stress down as a reason for being off sick - I wouldn't give her that satisfaction so I think it made her uncomfortable to question me about it. She was almost pleading with me to take up the counselling service and asking if there was any way she or anyone else could help. Perhaps I should have asked to see Pete - that might have put her in her place. No, I couldn't speak to Pete, alone, in a separate room like this. It was bad enough trying to answer the occasional off-hand questions as he passed by my desk. I sensed him hovering in the background one time, when I was on the receiving end of some regular verbal abuse, from a customer. As usual, I was sat there, being completely ineffectual, until Lyn showed up and took over. I supposed, with regret, that Pete rated Lyn as highly as everyone else seemed to.

Why do I let Pete dominate my thoughts, so much? He wouldn't ever consider me as girlfriend material, any more than the girls had ever really regarded me as one of their friends. Very occasionally I dare to sit at the same table at tea breaks, but I feel more and more excluded.
Stella exacerbated this isolation, by asking me specific questions, like if I had had a good week-end! Didn't she realise that I had absolutely no social life outside of work? I sometimes wonder if I should be making sure to never ever sit with them again, but I am still inexplicably drawn to them, like a magnet.

Pippa.

Oh My God! Wow, what the hell…I had actually been invited for an interview! I reckoned half the office probably thought I wasn't executive officer material, but I totally didn't care - I was going to give it my best shot. Pete was being dead sweet, saying he would help me prepare for the interview, but I didn't want to be too indebted to him. We'd had fun, but he was getting way too serious for my liking. He wanted to stay over, more and more. Initially I encouraged this, preferring the privacy of my flat, to that of the house he shared with two mates, who acted like over grown school boys, whenever we were there. Sex with Pete was good and getting better, but not brilliant. There was something innocent about him, though and I didn't want to hurt him.

Pete gave the impression he would be quite happy to be a permanent fixture in my flat. I had tried to imagine this, unsuccessfully and I missed my independence - the freedom to suit myself, at week-ends, go out with my mates, more. He was decent, sweet and considerate, but something was missing. I guess it was like he was too kind, too dependable and altogether too predictable. No, I needed someone to keep me on my toes, someone that gave me a challenge. Maybe I would let Pete help me prep for the interview, a bit, but I wouldn't go out with him that much longer, whether I got the promotion , or not. Nan would be disappointed, as she had really taken to him. What the hell though, I was too young to settle down and that's what he probably wanted.

I'm not quite sure how or why we agreed to go but it was a bit of a laugh going to Stella's church meeting with Lyn. Mind, it freaked me out a bit, when several people went up to the front to be saved by Jesus, or some such thing. Chatting to Lyn afterwards, we both agreed there had been some kind of atmosphere, there, probably mixed with our own tension. Lyn reckoned it was peoples' hopes and fears that inspired them and not necessarily a leap of faith. Trying to analyse it all, made me feel a bit uncomfortable and I decided that I didn't want to think about it, too much, otherwise it might turn me against Stella. It was all a bit weird but she was a good kid and a good mate. I never felt like I had to impress her or anything, we just had a totally good laugh.

Lyn seemed to deal with the whole religious stuff better than me. Even though she admitted to being slightly fazed at the conversions or whatever, she didn't appear too bothered afterwards. I reckoned she had everything going for her with her family, hubby and all. I knew that she was still close to her Mum, Dad and sisters and that they all got together quite a lot with family on both hers and Richard's side. I envied her that, but knew that my old Nan loved me enough to be sort of, like, a whole family. However, the security that Lyn had - I guessed maybe I would want this in the future. For now though, I just wanted to enjoy life - not to be sorted, not to be questioning life, not to be searching for any deep meaning - but just to be having some fun! Shit, you're only young once.

Debbie.

How I wished Pippa would stop taking any opportunity to belittle me!
How I wished Lyn would stop watching me! She is always hovering by my desk, even if someone merely raises their voice, now. She never watches Kate, Pippa or Stella, in the same way. I feel humiliated and paranoid. Paranoid that everyone thinks I'm stupid and neurotic. Why can't I cope, like the others? Kate gets cross with me, but at least I can share a bit of what I go through with her, even though I know she will be dismissive, cruel and sarcastic, in return. I try to emulate this hard, uncaring front she portrays to the world and wonder if that is all it is with her - a front.

I spend many hours, alone at home, analysing my friends. Not that they were my friends, of course, any more. Perhaps Lyn isn't as happy or as popular, as I thought. Maybe Kate and Pippa are both putting on an act and neither of them is actually that confident. Could Stella with her religion, even be considered a bit out of the ordinary? I hate it, that I can't be more like them and I despise myself for being so weak. I despise the sight of my four bedroom walls because I spend so much time in there and I hate my life.

I cannot risk even going into town at the weekend, in case I see them and they see that I am on my own. I know it's a big city, but it would be typical that I would see someone from work, so shopping or window shopping is out of the question. I have to live everything second hand through

Facebook and Twitter and wish for things that I could become a part of. My daydreams of Pete continue, but the irony and futility of this envelope me with a deeper and bleaker depression.

I find it harder and harder to get to sleep at night, so write in my haphazard diary, to try and stop the turmoil of thoughts tormenting me, with endless unanswerable questions. I cannot seem to switch off completely into fantasy mode anymore where I daydreamed of my life being different. If only I could believe in something - anything. The dread of what is yet to happen continues to lurk in my mind; an ever present dark and menacing shadow frightening and mocking me; preventing any rational thought.

If only I didn't feel ill, really ill, all the time. I'm so very tired all the time, but I can't ever seem to get more than a few hours' sleep in a night. Mum had asked me again to see the doctor - but my many and varied symptoms were confused. Sometimes, complete lethargy and a total inability to think or function and other times, a racing of the heart, profuse sweating and an overwhelming feeling of nausea, combined with utter blind panic. I also seemed to have a permanent headache now and painkillers only relieve this on a temporary basis. It angered me to assume that this may all just be anxiety. Surely all of this couldn't be down to stress alone?

Lyn.

I felt so helpless about Debbie. She was obviously really mega-stressed out and I couldn't get her out of my mind. So much so, I found myself talking about her again, with Rich, at home.

"Sweetheart" he reassured me "You've done everything you can by the sound of it. You've told Pete, as well - so he should be shouldering some of the responsibility."

I considered this and replied

"Well he has tried chatting to her, informally, but never gets anywhere. He is saying that we will have to start disciplinary procedures."

"I wonder why she doesn't just resign." Rich said "she obviously isn't cut out to work in a Dole Office."

I laughed at his terminology.

"How many times do I have to tell you? It hasn't been called that for years. It's a job centre, darling. No one calls it the Dole Office now. "

"Yeah. Whatever. A lot of people still think the Dole is where you sign on and the job centre is where you go for jobs." he returned. "Anyway the point is that it's only a job and surely it's not worth getting in a flunk about. If ever you wanted to look for another job, I'd back you all the way."

This made me think once again - why was I still there? I could probably get something else - and probably get more money. The wages were crap and Pete had implied that Jess, the replacement for Dawn, had been promised the job of Manager, even before the interviews had taken place. What was that all about? I thought about that John Lennon line in a song "life is what happens to you when you're busy making other plans" and decided two things. One - always appreciate and make the most of what you have. Two - try and change anything that's not working. Forget the recession, I had to try and change things for myself and find another job.

I wasn't going to get wound up about Pippa though. Some people were implying it was a foregone conclusion that she would be promoted to be a Supervisor, as it was just Pete and Jerry doing the interviews. I reminded them that Pippa had got this far on the strength of her work in her previous office, not just this one. So, she had only been here just about a year. The important thing was that she would be great in the job and God knows that was what was needed. I know she seemed a bit black and white and maybe a little arrogant, but I had listened to her dealing with customers on numerous occasions and she never failed to impress. She just had that thing of treating people as they would want to be treated, particularly in a one to one situation. She somehow made people feel special, whilst still being ultra-efficient, which was a rare combination. I wondered, not for the first time, whether her arrogance was covering up some deep-seated insecurity. After all losing her Mum when she was so young and never knowing her Dad must have taken its toll on her? Of course most of the staff didn't know about the hardships of Pippa's early life.

Throughout my many years of working in job centres, I had seen all sorts. Some colleagues had been very efficient but uncaring, some complete jobs- worth types, some really stressed or some completely indifferent, others lovely but lazy and others, like Pippa, who got nearly everything right. Stella was a more obvious candidate for getting everything right - particularly around the people skills stuff, but she lacked the confidence and experience that Pippa had. Privately I knew I was also damn good at dealing with the public and pretty good at dealing with everything to do with this job. As time went by though, I felt that I had to work at maintaining that level and I was getting tired of it. Also the checks and the petty bureaucracy seemed to have got worse over the years and with fewer staff it was getting harder and harder to provide a good service to the public.

However, we had such characters, over the years on both sides of the counter and it was all the laughs we had that had probably kept me here. Even potentially abusive situations ended up being funny sometimes. Some of the incidents were when staff had argued back with the Jobseekers or when staff had taken the option of not pursuing something when perhaps they should have done. "Yeah, ok am I bothered?" was a response uttered more than once, from either side.

I was laughing less and less though and perhaps my ability to always bounce back was diminishing. I knew when Rich and I were first together; I almost felt that I had to prove myself to him - that I was successful and independent in some way. As time went on though, I had come to realise that I didn't need to do this and actually I was only trying to prove my own worth to myself. I knew I could stretch myself more, I knew I was capable of gaining further promotion, but I also knew that I was happy to delude myself with the idea that I could do more, without ever actually pursuing it.

I would start looking for other jobs, as things weren't the same at work. We did have some fun, but there was more and more to do and less and less staff. Everyone saw me as being so chilled out whereas I knew that I was getting a bit stressed too. Not that I would admit it to anyone, of course. Having a case like Debbie, gave me more stress when she was in, what with all the monitoring and her looks of pure hatred in my direction. Indeed, I was secretly relieved, now, when she phoned in sick, which was a fairly regular occurrence.

So I was probably selfish but all I wanted was an easy life. Family and friends were what mattered, surely not work.

Debbie

Mum is beginning to look at me like the girls at work, now. I can't stand it anymore, the pity in everyone's eyes! I try to stay in my bedroom as much as possible, to avoid any communication. The trouble is I can't stop myself checking Facebook every five minutes, scrutinising their conversations, profiles and groups. Naturally they are all having a great time, not one of them has a care in the world and life is just one long party! I scan through some of the other people I don't know that well at work and the story is always the same - full on and so smug. Smiling drunk faces on all their posing pictures.

I told Mum I had been to the Doctor, just to shut her up. If she really cared, she would've asked me more about what was wrong, but she seemed relieved not to have to pursue the conversation, when I told her I had a virus. I was surprised how easy it was to lie. Although I thought I was lying - who knows, maybe I have got some strange virus? My physical symptoms come and go but I rarely feel anything approaching well. Maybe it is a virus that stops me coping, that makes me so desperate, an illness that makes me feel worthless and so alone.

Sometimes, I can't believe that I will ever have the courage to return to work. I have stayed at home for the last four days, staring again at my bedroom walls, so tired, but getting no sleep. My only existence is through my laptop and my only refuge is to think back a year, to when I first met Lyn, Kate, Pippa and Stella. Obviously, I had been extremely nervous, but I was part of the group, I was so close to making friends. Where had it all gone wrong? Had my expectations been too high? Why couldn't I be like other people just living and enjoying their lives. I had no life myself, I was just observing and analysing. My head felt too full and too tormented. If only I could rest or sleep. If only I had something, anything, to look forward to.

I knew with certainty, for example, that I would never have any chance with Pete - although actually just the sight of him at work, gave me a slight temporary lift. No, my big mistake was to think that I could be part of a group of friends; my mistake was to think that I wouldn't be on my own any more. Even though Kate still gave me slight hope of some kind of friendship; I still felt alone.

I had been alone all my life. Somehow I thought everything was going to change when I started this job. I felt I had been immediately accepted into a group of friends and my mistake was to assume that we were all actual friends; that we would all stay friends.

Stella

I knew Pippa must have passed the interview, when Lyn came over, waving an envelope towards her, with a huge grin on her face.

"You've done it!" I exclaimed.

Pippa tore open the envelope and quickly scanned the writing.

"I've got it! Oh My God! Jesus! Shit, shit, shit! I've been promoted!"

I looked around the rest of the office and sensed some disapproval, so pulled Pippa and Lyn towards me for a big hug.

"Less of the blaspheming" I joked, "and let's go out on Saturday - girls' night out, but just the three of us and really celebrate!"

They both agreed, with enthusiasm. I wondered if Pippa realised how some of the others kind of resented her and if she did, if it upset her? I think they were probably jealous and I always stuck up for her, if anyone was critical of her, when she wasn't around. I knew that Lyn also countered any bitchiness about Pippa and really respected her for it.

I enjoyed the evenings when we went out in a big crowd from the office and over the last few months there had been several more nights out for leaving do's as various colleagues escaped into other jobs. No guys that I thought were fit, which was a shame but then I knew my options were difficult; as they would have to share my faith. I had made some great friends though.

However Pippa and Lyn were really the only two individuals that I knew I had become close, good friends with. We all had such a laugh and they were fine about my faith, church and church friends. Admittedly the two paths didn't cross over that often, but much as I loved and prayed for my faithless family, I so now felt the same about Lyn and Pippa. I felt pretty sure they would both do anything for me and that they would both be long term friends. I still wished that they could understand and even share my spiritual life, but at least they hadn't condemned it all completely out of hand and thankfully the snide comments and jokes were now few and far between.

I have become accepted at the Youth Club where I go and help out now twice a week and it's good to be with youngsters who want to be where they are - so unlike all the jobseekers I interview at work. Obviously no-one wants to be signing on and although it's great when you might sort of help someone to find a job, mostly they don't want to engage with you and actually resent you, which I can understand.

It still really bugs me though that some staff - the ones typically who had been around a lot longer than me, can be so uncaring and judgemental. I'm not sure if it's complacency or just plain ignorance, but in some cases they deserve half the abuse that comes their way. Why won't everyone look for the good in others and at least show some respect for their fellow human beings?

Debbie

I must always remember that the anticipation of something is often worse than the actuality. I managed to go back into work on the Friday, following four straight days off, thinking that it was only one day to get through, until the weekend. However, after the initial heart- churning half an hour, I felt sort of ok and probably no worse, than if I had been at home. Lyn hadn't pounced on me as yet and Stella had asked if I was feeling better. The big news of the week had been that Pippa had got her promotion.

Kate was predictably livid, telling me that she was only successful because she had slept with Pete. Kate reckoned that a lot of other staff thought the same and wouldn't want to work under her. Although we were completely chalk and cheese, I still felt bizarrely that I had some sort of ally in Kate. I was able to talk to her when there was no way I would talk to the others. She still stuck up for me against Lyn doing all her monitoring and tried to reason with me about some of my negativity and anxiety. The fact that she was so cold and sarcastic did not matter too much to me - I just liked her honesty and wished I could share her resolute outlook on life.

Of course I wondered if Kate was so against Pippa because she was jealous of her seeing Pete. No matter how hard I tried, I couldn't stop torturing myself by imagining them together. I supposed I had known it was ridiculous to ever entertain fantasies involving Pete and me.
However, although I became immediately tongue-tied, I was still secretly pleased when Pete stopped by my desk.

118

He started with a routine
 "Glad to see you back."
He then proceeded to say that if I wanted to talk to him
about anything, I could. He continued that he
"Knew how it was a very stressful job and that it was good
step to recognise this."
For a fleeting moment, it crossed my mind that he was
saying the same things as Lyn, but I soon dismissed that,
preferring to think that he genuinely cared about me and
wasn't just talking as a Manager.

After he had moved away from my desk, I noticed he had
left a leaflet about Counselling Services and "Coping with
Stress". It was the very same leaflet that Lyn had given
me in our last interview.

Pippa

I went round to see Nan after work on the day I was told that I had been promoted. She was totally tickled pink. She wrote down Executive Officer on her note pad by the phone to remind her to tell anyone and everyone that her grand-daughter was doing so well in her Civil Service career!

"You make it sound much better than it is, Nan" I admonished her gently.

"Nonsense my gal" she returned. "You've done well for yourself and no mistake. Your own flat and being an *Executive Officer* and you're still only twenty five - a slip of a gal!"

I couldn't help smiling. I reckoned Nan would be proud of me whatever I did, but I would make a go of this, work my way up and see that I gave her good cause to be, like, real chuffed.

I guessed that some of the older staff would be a bit pissed off that I had got my promotion, but to hell with them. I knew I was young and a bit too self-assured, but I knew I got stuff done and didn't get all stressed like most of them. Yeah it was a pain of a job a lot of the time and people had a go at you, but you could have a laugh and I knew the pay I would get on promotion was actually way up on what some of my old school friends were still on.

Stella, Lyn and I had a great night out the following Saturday. Double JDs and cokes all night and a cab ride booked to take us home. So much so, that I was telling them both I wasn't completely sure I wanted to take the promotion, as it would mean moving to another section, based on the other floor. I knew it was only work, but we all got on so well, I knew I would miss them during the day. Stella laughed.

"We will still see you in the tea room, unless you're planning to work right through!" This was followed by more laughter.

"I'm sure there's no danger of that." Lyn said "and you and I will have the pleasure of attending the Supervisors meetings, together, every fortnight."

Lyn had been brilliant. Not only had she encouraged me to go for the job, she had convinced me I would be really good in the role. I knew a lot of people probably thought I was a right cocky cow, but I would prove them wrong. Sod them anyway. I wondered what everyone would think if I split up with Pete - this was the first bridge to cross I guess. I voiced my thoughts out loud, to which Lyn and Stella looked quite surprised.

"Is this the alcohol talking?" Lyn asked "I thought you two were getting quite serious"

"I did really like him, at first." I answered "but he was getting way too serious"

"Well if you do finish with him, do you care what other people think?" Stella queried.

"No - I guess not, not if you're both cool with it" I replied. We all laughed and they didn't need to spell anything out, they were good mates and I reckoned always would be.

I still had friends from school and college that I hooked up with, but I felt a lot closer to Stella and Lyn. Not that I would admit it to them but I reckoned I could be more myself somehow; not be so guarded or quite so cocky!

Well weird; I felt I could rely on them and perhaps even trust them. God, what serious soppy thoughts, I chided myself. Must be one or two JDs and coke too many!

The rest of the evening we drank, we giggled and we drank some more.

Debbie

Somehow I had managed to keep coming into work, although I had ceased to feel any fragment of friendship with the others. I had started taking all of my tea breaks earlier to avoid sitting with them and found that occasionally Kate had decided to do the same.
"God, I thought Lyn was bad enough as a Supervisor," she moaned "but imagine working for that slag Pippa!"
I didn't say anything, but felt a tight smile around my lips. I had often thought that Kate and Pippa were quite similar in some ways. They were both so sure of themselves, so sure in their opinions and of their place in the world. So much the opposite of what I was like, so much of what I yearned to be like, myself.

I had come to the realisation that being at work was better than being at home - somehow I didn't feel quite so frightened or alone. Not that I was part of any thing here, but maybe I was still on the fringes. The difficulty was not just trying to fit in socially, but also coping with the customers. I don't know how the others could joke so much about the abuse, the foul language and the threats - it simply scared me, on each and every occasion. The hovering security guard never seemed to be a deterrent. Whilst they shouted and gesticulated, I shrank and I shook, until typically Lyn came and took over. Recently, even Pippa had intervened one time - no doubt practising for when she started properly as a new Supervisor.

There is hardly ever any respite from seeing clients for their signing on. Occasionally, a few of us less experienced staff are herded off into the training room to complete on line courses or to get some workshop style training. The former provides an unusual chance to relax for an hour or so. The latter is fraught with new and different anxieties. Will the tutor insist on those tortuous role-play exercises? Will I be singled out to share an opinion? Will I have to introduce the person sat next to me? Will it start off with one of those ridiculous ice breakers - a complete contradiction of terms if ever I had heard one.

How I wish I could be detached like some of the other staff. They obviously saw an opportunity to have a laugh, have a moan, or in one case actually have a nap! The chap, who fell asleep, to the extent he was actually snoring, was teased endlessly afterwards, but the trainer was too embarrassed or too lazy to do anything about it at the time, during the session. Again this was a source of great hilarity among the other staff; I saw Kate and Stella laughing, but I didn't understand the humour. What was so funny about someone falling asleep in a training session, when you were meant to be learning things for work?

Kate

Although it was the gossip of the Office, Pippa dumping Pete did not bring her as much grief, as she deserved. Fucking hell, didn't they know what she was like and what she'd done? So as soon as she had got her promotion, she dumps him. What a manipulative bitch, how could she get away with it? I know Debbie hates her as well, by the way she looks at her, but not that she would ever say so.

What gets me is how matey Stella and Lyn are with her. They are all so full of themselves, thinking that they are the centre of attention. Of course Debbie's so needy and impressionable; she still well, wants to be a part of the gang. The silly cow wants to be liked and seeks their approval, whenever she has the temerity to open her stupid mouth. Why she won't listen to me, I don't know. She hates Lyn for going on about her sickness, she's jealous of Pippa for screwing Pete and she resents Stella for being good friends with them both, when she should have been the odd one out; what with her religion and all that rubbish.

I can see them all for what they are - smug and self-interested and not worth knowing really. They are all the same. They are all as bad as each other. I just hope I never have to work for that slag Pippa. I think a lot of the other staff reckoned she slept with Pete to get her promotion, but they're too damn wimpy to say anything. When I look around at the other people in this dump, I wonder how anything ever gets done. Half the people in charge are such a bunch of losers - jobs-worth nerdy types who take themselves way too seriously and then the self - obsessed bull-shitters who blag their way through life, getting what they want -whatever the cost. Jerry was the worst of the lot, a complete prat who thought he was something special, just because he was the boss! Most of the rest of the office staff are wimps and weirdoes who can't cope with the jobseekers or the rest of the work.

How totally superficial it was of Pippa to dump Pete pretty well straight away, though. Poor sod, at least he was one of the few who were ok with the work and all that. He wasn't a wimp; but just stupid, to be taken in by that bitch. Damn it; I'm really going to avoid her as much as possible so she can't keep getting on my nerves.

One of these days she will get what she deserves, she will get her come-uppance, I thought grimly.

Debbie

If only I could think more like Kate! I know what she says makes sense, but she's so callous, so mean, but so probably right. Perhaps I could get on with my life, if they ceased to matter to me? Poor Pete was going round looking very down and the rumour was that he would do anything to have Pippa back. Pippa meanwhile has continued to strut around the place, without a care in the world. How could she be so mean and callous? Why did she go out with him in the first place if she didn't really like him? Why did it matter to me so much though and why did I still yearn to be her friend, now she had treated Pete so badly?

There was never any suggestion now of nights out or even lunchtimes up at the local, but I supposed my going to tea breaks at earlier times avoided the potential of conversations leading to such possibilities. Once in a while I mustered the courage to wait a while and relive the early days of when we had all sat together. It was so bittersweet, such moments of irony as on these rare occasions, when I laughed along with them. How I picked up on the rest of the staff listening in on our conversations, how I still occasionally basked in the reflected glory of sharing the old table in the tea room with the in crowd.

I also understood dimly that other people in the office got stressed out. Listening in to other conversations in the tea room made me realise that a lot of them were trying to get other jobs and hated a lot of what we were supposed to do. Surprisingly though this wasn't always just about having to deal with angry clients but often about all the paperwork and procedures. I knew of people getting into trouble over leaving files out on their desk or forgetting a document left in the photocopier and even a supervisor who was on a warning about letting someone else access her computer. These all seemed quite minor things to me and it made me think that my sickness record would definitely be considered even more seriously. Staff who had been around for a long time complained that there was a lot more bureaucracy and more of an atmosphere of fear rather than fun.

Nadia, who hated dealing with jobseekers, said that that wasn't as bad now as all the pressure to reach targets and get all the paperwork right. It was quite something coming from her, I thought. I remembered that she had had to deal with racist comments and threats worse than I had ever had and felt sorry for her. I supposed this should have made me feel a bit less helpless and insecure, but it didn't.

My grasp on reality was slim, I realised this, but any small measure of excitement, sustained me, however briefly and however anxious it rendered me. Pete hardly came out of his office since Pippa had finished with him, so I had no opportunity to day dream of a glimpse of happiness, following our occasional chats together. Perhaps in time Pete would see Pippa for what she was and view her in the same way that Kate did. He probably wouldn't go for someone like Kate though, because she was too similar to Pippa. Perhaps in time he might view me as a friend. Perhaps in time I would get a life. Who was I kidding; there was no more hope of Pete liking me, than there was of all my anxieties going for good.

Lyn.

I didn't realise how happy I could be, until today. The sparkling shining light in Rich's eyes assured me that he was equally ecstatic.

"We're going to have a baby!" he exclaimed.

I kissed him again and again and once more felt an immense gratitude for the life I had, Rich, our family and our friends. I couldn't quite believe that this happiness knew no bounds and that I would soon be a mother - that Rich and I had created a new life -wow - that this new life would be a part of both of us and that we would continue on through this new life. It was a bit scary but so exciting, so unbelievable and so fantastic!

It occurred to me that I hadn't realised how much this would mean to me. I had come off the Pill nearly a year ago, as we had both wanted to have children, but we had been quite pragmatic about it. It really hadn't bothered me when I had continued to have my period each month and I had thought if I never fell pregnant it wouldn't have been a big deal. Now I wasn't so sure; this was a hell of a big deal and Rich was excitedly going through when and where we would share our good news with our families and friends. It made me smile to think of Mum and Dad; they would be so happy for us and I guessed they would love being grandparents.

"Also you should definitely give up work now – no question about it" he concluded.

"One step at a time, sweetheart" I replied.

"I can get maternity leave for starters and maybe I could go back on a part time basis. That wouldn't be so bad - there are some advantages to working there you know."

"Whatever you want to do, darling" and he started kissing me, again.

I wondered then why I was even suggesting staying on. Maybe it was to test him out? I was pretty sure that a little part of my joy was thinking it was a way of getting out of work. The baby was incredible, awesome and very sobering; leaving the job centre by contrast would be easy and more than anything, a relief. My mind was running away thinking of all the good stuff that would be happening over the next few months and the next few years. None of this speculation included working in a job centre!

I couldn't believe the extent of the excitement I felt. I knew I felt nervous too; but nervous in a good way and just so happy. I couldn't stop smiling and being thankful for my life - the family and friends that our baby would be welcomed into. Life was random; I was lucky.

Debbie.

I suppose I should have been pleased for Lyn.

Announcing her pregnancy, she appeared genuinely awe struck and grateful. I just couldn't help thinking how some people had all the luck. She was the typical woman who had it all. Why was life so unfair and so haphazard in the allocation of happiness?

Stella was hugging Lyn when Pippa asked:

"Was it planned?"

There was a perceptible pause and then Lyn answered.

"Yeah, pretty very much so and now it's happened, I've realised just how much this means to me."

"Fair play" Pippa replied "I just can't imagine you with kids though, babe."

Stella started laughing and said

"More like you can't imagine yourself with children."

I tried to imagine having children, myself. I knew of course that this was an absolute impossibility. Kate voiced her somewhat predictable opinion to me later.

"I wouldn't be surprised if it was an accident and now she's trying to make the most of it."

I wasn't sure if I agreed with her, but allowed myself a half smile at the possibility of her suggestion. I had to convince myself that other people might have problems, too. Maybe even Pippa secretly wanted to have kids. As always, though, I knew what I felt and how I felt, was beyond the usual worries or everyday problems of others. My anxiety was so intense and so continual.

I found it hard to imagine what would be happening to me in about a week's time; so genuinely couldn't foresee a future beyond my current and immediate anxieties. The overwhelming sense of barely coping with the drowning oppression of having to go to work or being alone in my room at home. I had very little respite now between bouts of real actual panic and being able to function normally. Normal: what was that? Was the definition of normal to be Lyn with her husband and baby on the way, Stella with her God or Pippa and Kate with their larger than life attitude?

I would take anything; I believed I would make a deal with God if only he took my stress away; I could cope if only I had a family or one person that loved me. More than anything though, I thought I could just carry on, just live a life, if I could believe a little bit in myself. If only I had half the self-assurance of Kate or Pippa; I could keep going.

Stella.

I was dead chuffed for Lyn, who seemed so pleased at the news of her pregnancy. However, it did make me start thinking about the job again. One of the main reasons I was still working in the job centre, was the friendships I had formed. I did feel that I made a difference with the jobseekers, sometimes, too. However, Pippa would be moving to another section soon, as a new supervisor and Lyn would be off on maternity leave and then maybe for good. These two were the friends that meant the most to me and I felt that I would stay in touch with them, even if we weren't all working together.

I knew I had sort of gained good experience and life skills through this job, over the last year. The Youth Club was good fun and I was surprised that it hadn't taken too long for most of them to come round. I think they respected me for just listening to them and I knew that listening to Jobseekers had probably helped me to relate with people of all ages in general. Looking ahead though, I knew there was no way I wanted to still be here for too much longer. I didn't want to end up like some of the older staff who hated the work but felt they couldn't leave. I certainly didn't want to become as cynical as some by viewing everyone that signed on in the same poor light and ceasing to treat them as individuals.

I know that Pippa found it a bit of a laugh when some of the more long term staff moaned about the job, but I could see how it would be quite easy to end up like them. After all there was quite a lot of kind of ridiculous rules and regulations that seemed to get in the way of spending time helping clients with their job search. I know it was easy enough to complain about everything, but sometimes I just thought of how we looked to the poor people who were signing on.

It bugged me when staff meetings were called last minute and we had to make do with a hastily scrawled apology going up on the front door to warn all the customers that we would be opening late that morning. On one occasion we must have kept them waiting over half an hour and Tim the poor security guard was tasked with placating the small crowd that converged in the doorway, until he was allowed to let them in.

I thought some people saw me as a bit naïve and sort of soft for sticking up for the clients, but secretly I also dreaded interviewing certain people who upset or frightened me. I felt ashamed for not being able to help the ones who obviously had mental health issues and so shouldn't really have been signing on in the first place. I thought what we offered was never enough and I felt that I should be able to relate more. I had surprised myself by being able to relate to the kids at the Youth Club, but I wished I could do this as well at work.

I also wished that I had Lyn's strength to challenge the odd few who were playing the system.
"So is that going to help you get a job then?" She had asked one rough looking young lad who was proudly displaying his newly tattooed knuckles spelling f-u-c-k and o-f-f-!

"Better than l-o-v-e and h-a-t-e though innit?" He had sneered. Well what could you do but laugh.

I so needed and wanted a job that made more of a difference. I wanted to help people, without getting tied up in paperwork and politics. Use my Art somehow and not be so conventional. Work for a charity full time or something like that. I needed something more vocational or spiritual, to challenge and to fulfil me. Once I had come to this realisation, I decided to start looking at applying for other jobs, straight away. I thanked God that the next chapter in my life would be starting soon....

Debbie.

So I wake up in the morning, feeling sick. The overwhelming nausea remains throughout the day, intensifying during extra stressful moments. I struggle to control my breathing and my heart pounds hard and fast, without relief. I vacillate between feeling hot and sweaty to feeling shivery and almost numb with cold. The way I feel physically, pails into insignificance, compared to the torture in my mind.   I sometimes think I must be mad - insane and that nothing can ever change the nightmare existence of my life. I wonder what it is like to feel calm, happy, loved, secure, or even just a part of something and think that I will never ever experience such normality.

I try to remember the last time I ate a proper meal. Was it two weeks, three weeks ago? I can't really taste the food somehow and if any- one is watching me - well Mum or Dad - I struggle to chew and swallow. Alone in my room at home, I try to fight the growing and overwhelming panic. I decide I will have to resign from the job and start afresh. I must get out of the job centre. It is the work and the people there who have made me like this and made me worse than ever before. Even though Kate quite often came to tea breaks at the same time as me, she wasn't with me a lot the time and really I had to face the fact that I was alone. Surrounded by people, noise and frantic activity, but I was totally alone.

My room at home is not an escape or a safe haven though. My laptop on top of the cheap desk taunts me - full to brimming with the lives of others. I glimpse the lives of other people who display their packed social lives with friends; their control and their confidence. All those social networking sites are constantly proving to them just how social they are.

The austere single bed which I have had from the age of about four or five also screams rejection at me with tangled sheets and crumpled duvet evidence of my regular lack of sleep. The bedside lamp is old and basic casting a dim light over everything which is preferable to the loud glaring main light with a 100 watt bulb that I can't be bothered to change.
My small dressing table has sufficient room for my hair brush, the odd few bits of make -up and two bottles of cheap perfume that have lasted me nearly a year. The drawers in this and my single wardrobe house the paltry selection of clothes that I own. I have never been that interested in clothes and have never enjoyed shopping.

The odd few posters I dared to blu-tack to the walls as a teenager, now look dog-eared and old fashioned. The pop stars having been long since replaced with cooler new ones that I don't know enough about. The walls and ceiling close in on me to the extent that I cower under the duvet until I can slowly regain a proper pattern to my breathing.

My previous sense of foreboding has become much more intense. I keep thinking that things can't get any worse, but then they do and I remember overhearing Pete saying earlier to Lyn that I "really needed watching."
How could he turn against me like everyone else?

Pippa.

It was well weird having a serious work type conversation with Lyn. It concerned Debbie, of course. I knew she was in trouble for all the time she'd had off sick and I knew she was totally nervous around difficult customers, but I hadn't really connected the two things together. Lyn explained she was pretty certain Debbie's time off was all stress related and that she and Pete were quite worried about her. Pete hadn't ever said anything to me about Debbie, but then he'd hardly spoken to me, since we had split up.

I would be moving off to a new section, soon, to start as a Supervisor, but it seemed like Lyn was giving me a bit of a forewarning of what was involved. Chatting about Debbie made me realise that managing the staff could be like more difficult than dealing with the worst customers! I promised Lyn I would help to keep a bit of an eye on Debbie, but I was secretly pleased that she wasn't really my responsibility.

Lyn also warned me what the Supervisors' meetings would be like. She reckoned that some of them were totally out for themselves and that they liked to take the credit for everything whilst making sure they always covered for their mistakes.

"Yeah it can be a complete blame culture here sometimes you know," she said "but when the self - congratulation gets really obvious, some of us start to toot out mock trumpet blowing in the background to bring them down a peg or too. So it's not all mega-serious; but you have to be careful and watch what you say."

So although Lyn had tried to prepare me, it was still totally strange going to my first Supervisor's meeting. Although I knew no-one thought that much of Jerry, he dominated most of the conversations and Pete and Jess appeared to go along with everything he said. Pete tried not to look at me most of the time. It was all like, so serious and all the supervisors and advisors seemed a bit intimidated somehow. Jerry was such an idiot; he loved the sound of his own voice and talked about himself a lot of the time. I couldn't get why the others seemed too scared to challenge him on anything but I thought of what Lyn had said and kept my mouth shut. I reckoned I would just have to bide my time; get used to him and not question any stuff too soon.

There were a few times though, that things got, like, quite confused. There was a lot of talk about some new booking system that sounded complete crap but we were going to have to use it, regardless. Then Jerry was talking about some sort of "Suicide Policy" and Lyn asked if it was for staff. A few people giggled but I could tell that this time Lyn hadn't actually been joking. She must be thinking of some member of staff that was way screwed up, I thought. Probably Debbie I reckoned, although there were a few other likely candidates. I knew a couple of older staff were off long-term with work type stress.

I struggled to stay focused for the rest of the meeting. There was loads of other stuff about customer policies and procedures. Then there was more about compliance and checks and other such rubbish. Oh my God, I hadn't really expected all of this.

I suddenly remembered a tale Lyn had told me about one of her friends being offered a temporary promotion, a few years back. Apparently she had replied something like "No thanks, I would rather stand in a bucket of shit!" I was beginning to see her point.

Debbie.

I feel like a robot, going through automatic responses - verbally and physically. I've decided to give it one more month and if I still feel like hell, I will resign. Anyway, why wait for them to sack me? There's just no way that I couldn't feel a bit better if I left this job - not only to get away from dealing with the public, but also to be able to completely sever all ties with the others. I don't know how I ever imagined that they could have been my friends, how on earth could I have kidded myself, that much?

Pippa and Lyn are all matey now going off to their management meetings.
I hate it every time one of them looks at me or worse still tries to engage me in conversation. I hate witnessing their self-satisfied smiling faces, I hate listening to their smug stories and I despise their confidence and sense of belonging.

Time and time again, I wondered what made me so different, so isolated and so apart from others. Every time I go in the tea room, I keep my head down and try to avoid any eye contact. I avoid sitting with anyone whenever possible and always pick up a magazine to bury my head in. Sometimes I get my phone out to try and look preoccupied, but every time I look through Facebook or Twitter it confirms my lack of status, lack of worth and my invisibility. Sometimes I pretend to be responding to a text that I have never received and sometimes I pretend to be accessing my voicemail when I know there are no messages there for me.

141

Sometimes I don't take a break at all, but then I have the continued threat and hell of seeing job seekers; one after another, one after another, without pause and all of them potential psychos as Kate would delight in saying.

Where is my respite, where is my refuge? Certainly not at home, I thought.

Even Mum and Dad seemed remote and disinterested. God, if no-one else loves me, they should, at least, I thought. They were so old; I supposed that I had been a mistake, an accident, as nothing was ever said to make me feel to the contrary. What about orphans then - were they in the same acute turmoil as me? Someone, somewhere in the world, maybe was this miserable, but that didn't make me feel any better. I really doubted that anyone could feel quite as anxious or as worthless as I did, right now.

Kate.

I think I'm going to have to steer clear of Debbie, who is getting more and more mad and neurotic. How many times have I tried to reason with the stupid bitch? "What have you got to be worried about?" I ask her. I keep telling her not to be so damn sensitive all the time. Christ, does she think she's the only one in the world with problems? Not that I can see what her problems are at any rate; it's all inside her head and she's just plain jealous of the so called cool gang. At least when I still sat with the others then the breaks were a bit of a laugh, but Pippa really did get on my nerves most of the time.

Of course someone like Pippa is always going to be a pain in the ass, even though she's on another section now. Mind you, Lyn can get on your nerves too, but why let it get to you? Pippa was probably strutting around the place getting on everyone's nerves. She could soon come unstuck though, I hoped. As a supervisor she would have to see all the crappy jobseekers that kicked off and then they had to help out when it was well busy. She's now got more responsibility, like Lyn, and everything gets to her, so it would be just great to see Pippa lose control and flip or fail.

I sometimes watched Lyn after she'd dealt with an angry client and I knew she was just putting on a carefree confident act. Well it didn't fool me and I reckoned she got stressed out like half the other staff in this madhouse. Someone like Stella was probably putting on an act half the time, too. How could anyone be so damn understanding and patient with the jobseekers? Yeah, she gave the impression of really wanting to help, but I could see right through that. She was after an easy life and didn't want to face up to challenging anyone because she didn't want to be shouted at!

I supposed there was no way Debbie was ever going to cope here; not with the work; not with anything. Fuck knows how she ever expected to make friends or get a life. She was a loser, a loner, a mouse who got the life she deserved. I don't suppose she would ever be able to see herself from the outside like I could. She was so well wrapped up in herself; being so shit scared and all that; it was selfish.

Debbie couldn't see that all her angst and jealousy was eating her up and making her crazy. Well, I wasn't going to be the one to calm her down, boost her up or share her insecurities. She could carry on wallowing in self -pity as far as I was concerned; as long as she left me out of it. She was just getting way too strange and I guessed she could be booted out of this job pretty soon now, although the stupid cow probably didn't have a clue that was on the cards.

Debbie.

Each time a new customer sits in front of me, at my desk, I take a deep breath and try to think of them as a ray of light or a glimmer of hope. This time could it be different, could I connect with someone, or, if they get angry, could I cope and calm them down? There was one after another and another one and another one. I wondered dimly how much more I could take. Then there was another and one after another. My trance like state wasn't calmness; it was simply registering the fact that I would never have any rest or any peace. There was one after another and another one and yet more waiting in the background.

Why couldn't I see them as individual people like Stella and to be honest, even Lyn did? Why couldn't I see that most of them didn't want to be here - that most of them would simply rather have a job? Why couldn't I sympathise with their plight; their diminishing hope and confidence; their suffocating mix of fear and bravado? No, they were just one after another and another one and another one. They were the treadmill of jobseekers; nameless and faceless as far as I was concerned, that had become an integral part of my desperation. One after another and another and another.

I was lost in these thoughts when the overweight tattooed man in front of me started shouting and shoving screwed up paper across the desk at me with big ugly fists. Dimly, I was aware of Kate suddenly screaming loudly, "Fuck off! Just fuck off! "

She then grabbed a pair of scissors on my desk. She seemed to be waving them in the direction of the customer, when Pippa came striding over. I hadn't been aware that she was even back on our section.

"Stop!" she yelled as she tried to grasp the scissors from Kate.

I felt oddly elated when I realised that Kate was actually thrusting the blades into Pippa's stomach and blood started to gush out from the wound. It was glorious, lovely deep dark red blood, soiling her pretty, pale lilac, shiny, silk blouse.

"God, Debbie" Pippa spluttered. "What have you done to me?"

I looked at her, trying to understand.

"It was Kate" I started to protest but my thoughts were all muddled.

The man with tattoos had come round to my side of the desk and was pulling me away from Pippa and he now seemed to be holding the bloodied scissors.

"Call the Police!" he yelled "She's a right psycho!"

Tim the security guard who was never around when you needed him had rushed over and seemed to grapple with me as well. Everyone else crowded around Pippa, the fallen heroine, as she crumbled to the floor.

Lyn.

As I strolled back in to the section, I knew immediately
something was wrong. A crowd had gathered near
Debbie's desk and I was horrified to see Pippa on the floor
clutching her stomach. She was covered in blood. I then
saw Tim and another man holding Debbie and assumed he
had attacked Pippa first. My hands instinctively went to
my own stomach and my heart lurched, thinking about my
unborn child.
"Please calm down. Let's talk." I began.
Many people were talking all at once,
"It was Debbie" they were saying. The burly jobseeker
still holding on to her joined in:
"Yeah, she tried to have a go at me first too, would you
believe it- the silly bitch, till this poor pretty girl tried to
stop her."
He gestured over to where Pippa was lying on the floor.

A wave of nausea swept over me, along with a cold stark
realisation that I wasn't somehow surprised - Debbie had
finally flipped. She seemed to be mumbling something
over and over like:
"It was Kate. Not me. Kate."
Stella in the meantime had rushed across all red faced and
breathless,
"An Ambulance and the Police are on their way - they will
be here soon." She then bent down next to Pippa and held
the hand which wasn't ineffectually clutching her wound.
Then the first aider, Rosie, arrived with a kit and took
over. There seemed to be so much blood, but Rosie
seemed to be saying reassuring things to her. Everything

was going in slow motion and my only real feelings were of physical sickness and an overwhelming sense of panic.

"Debbie" I said "What on earth have you done?"
"Why….." I continued but faltered; unable to articulate.
She looked at me vaguely quizzical and concerned, but with wild eyes.
"Why are these men holding me" she whimpered. "They have let Kate get away!"
I looked at her in despair and disbelief.
"You know what you have done; you have just stabbed Pippa! Why on earth are you talking about a Kate? Who the hell is Kate?"

Debbie.

I didn't understand what was happening. Why was I being restrained? Why wasn't anyone helping me? My head was thumping and my whole body was shaking, there were too many people crowding round and too much noise. There was always so much noise - inside and outside my head. I made a half- hearted attempt to break free, but Tim and the tattooed man held me even tighter. "Keep still, you crazy bitch" he snarled.

I caught Pippa looking at me with utter contempt, what was wrong with her, I thought. Then I remembered - good grief, it was all coming back to me. It was like watching a film in slow motion - Kate had stabbed her with a pair of scissors! I couldn't understand why that had happened. That's why Pippa was lying on the floor and why Rosie was holding a big bandage on her stomach.
"Are you ok" I asked nicely.
"What do you fucking care?" she spluttered back.
I looked around at the other staff and some of the public that were gawping at me. I perceived a mixture of incredulity and disgust on their faces.
"What are you looking at me for" I managed to question and asked
"What did Kate do and where has she gone?"

"Debbie, why do you keep talking about a Kate?" Lyn asked resignedly. "There is no-one called Kate here" she added.
Stella looked up at Lyn and then over at me.
"Oh Debbie" she sighed.

149

I registered some pity in her voice and eyes, bleakly, before she focused her attention back to Pippa.

Stella.

I found myself praying silently, for Pippa. I knew the wound couldn't be too bad – the scissors could be no more than 6 inches long and it had looked like Debbie had thrust it only once, or was it twice? It all seemed so unreal - as though I should wake up from a particularly hideous vivid nightmare. I was also asking God for strength, when I heard the sirens blaring outside. I overheard someone say "Great - at least they got here quickly; it's only been a few minutes."

It had seemed like an eternity to me! I became aware that Pippa had started to clutch my hand more tightly.

"Come with me to the hospital" she stuttered.

I smiled at her, trying to remain calm and reassuring; though I felt anything but.

"Well it's a better option than staying at work" I replied.

I was so pleased to see a sort of weak grin in response.

While the paramedics were checking over Pippa, I went to talk to Lyn. She looked very pale and really upset.

"Hey she'll be all right, you know" I started to say.

"Yes" she agreed "but it's all so horrible. I should've done something - Pete and I have been worried about Debbie for ages."

Lyn paused as we both came to the same realisation.

"Where is Pete - he probably doesn't even know Pippa's hurt - you should find him"

Lyn nodded and hurried back through the office as I returned to Pippa. "Lyn's gone to get Pete" I told her.

"That's all I need" she grimaced slightly, but I thought that she did want him at least to know; she had never admitted to herself quite how much she had liked this ordinary but decent guy. Probably one of the few guys she had hooked up with that wasn't an arrogant sod.

The paramedics got Pippa on to the stretcher and were carrying her out to the Ambulance when Pete arrived.
"God, Pippa, are you ok?" he asked.
"Do you want me to come with you?"
Pippa looked over at me and shook her head slowly and replied
"No don't bother, Stella's coming."
Pete touched my shoulder lightly and said
"Please look after her then and just don't worry at all about work. We will get cover for you, just stay with her, whatever and phone me. Please phone me as soon as she's seen a doctor."

Debbie.

The room I was sat in was cold and bare. A police woman had come in and left a cup of tea in front of me. I tried hard to think why I was here. What had happened? My mind was blank, but racing thoughts attempted to crack the void. My usual feelings of nausea and panic were strangely absent, but an overriding numbness now engulfed me. I felt like I had not slept for days or maybe weeks on end. My ever present acute anxiety and turmoil had abated though and I wondered if the big black cloud of looming uncertainty and danger had gone away for good.

A brisk efficient looking woman entered the room and sat opposite me. "You haven't drunk your tea" she chastised. "Hot sweet tea - good for shock" she continued.
I knew this woman wanted to talk to me, to find things out, but I also knew she was completely wasting her time. I didn't want to talk - not to anyone, so she could rabbit away all day, it would not make any difference.

Pippa.

After they had finished putting the stitches in, I was on my own for the first time since Debbie had stabbed me. This gave me time to, like, reflect. I tried to think back over the last year, to work out what had made her so mad. Oh My God! The pure hatred in her eyes as she pushed the scissors into me was just awful. Was it jealousy? Had she fancied Pete? Christ that was all over, though. Or when she had overheard me saying she was a bit weird? I guess I didn't really know what Debbie had thought. She was so quiet most of the time - one off funny sarcastic outbursts, but otherwise just shy. Maybe I had teased her a bit in the beginning. She had always been a bit strange and stressed out at work, but what did that have to do with me?

Was she envious that I had been promoted? No, she couldn't even handle what she was doing, so that couldn't be it. Was she jealous of my friends? Of course, I had started at the office on the same day as her and Stella - but then we had all gone out with Lyn a few times in the beginning. Debbie had just drifted off - going on breaks at different times, being off sick all the time and then she was always so quiet. She really struggled with the punters - God knows why she came to work in a job centre in the first place. Then, it occurred to me. Maybe it was just because I tried to take over when she lost it with that customer. She was actually screaming at him to "Fuck off" - so maybe he would have been stabbed, not me, if I hadn't intervened. He had looked a bit of an ugly old bastard but then you would think she would have got used

to the jobseekers by now. It just totally didn't make any
sense.

They had told me I shouldn't have too much of a scar, in
time, and that I would be able to go home, after a Doctor
had checked the stitching. It was, like, a bit of an anti-
climax, I was thinking as Stella returned to my bed side,
with two cups of coffee that looked like dishwater.
"Machine rubbish I'm afraid" she said.
"Do you want me to call your Nan?"
"No it will be better coming from me I reckon. I don't
want her to panic. Have you got my bag" I asked.
She rooted around under the bed and passed me my bag. I
took my phone out, but then placed it on the bedside table
and took Stella's hand.
"It's a good excuse for you to skive off work for the rest of
the day though - if you stay here with me?"
She returned my smile and had a gulp of her coffee.
"Yeah, it's no problem. Cool." she said. She seemed a bit
embarrassed that I was still sort of clutching her hand in
mine. I supposed it was a weird situation and it was hard
to be too serious when I wanted to thank her somehow but
couldn't, like, find the right words.
"Cool" I replied, letting go of her hand and picking up my
phone.

I knew Pete would want to come in to see me as soon as he
finished work; so I fired a quick text off telling him I was
fine; that my Nan would be coming in soon and that I
didn't like, want any other visitors yet. He would be great
at looking after me and being a good friend if that was all I
wanted, but I knew he just didn't rock my boat. I guessed
it would be better for him not to be mates at all really, but I

didn't want to sever all ties somehow and that was a bit weird. Rather than analyse it all too much though, I deliberately turned my thoughts elsewhere and rang my Nan. I kept my voice calm and played it all down as much as I could but Stella must have seen my eyes filling up and silently passed me a tissue.

Debbie.

It was strange how comfortable I felt in my silence. The woman pretended to be kind and caring, but I wouldn't talk. Then she got angry. Then she got dismissive. I daydreamt as she droned on and hugged myself in my silence. Cold, clear, still, silence. I shut my eyes but still I do not sleep; I never sleep.

Lyn.

I was so glad to get out of the office a bit earlier than normal and even more relieved to find Rich waiting in the Car Park for me. He looked pretty anxious striding up and down whilst tossing his car keys from one hand to the other. After we hugged, he searched my face and I felt his concern, his love. The relief flooded through me as I held on to him tight, not wanting to let go.

"You said Debbie was stressed out - but this is mad. Your job is mad. It's all crazy, you should just give it up, walk out now - we don't need the money."
It was just what I wanted to hear, but I think my phone call to him, a while ago, had probably made things sound worse than they were.
"Pippa is absolutely fine you know - Stella called from the Hospital. She's got her Nan with her now and she will be discharged tonight. I'm going round to see her later," I tried to reassure him.
"Darling, all I care about is you, but now we've got our baby to think about as well." He said, still anxious.
"Let's not make any hasty decisions." I said, hating the fact that I sounded so ridiculously sensible.

"After the baby comes, we can think about things again, then, job wise." I concluded. There was always something of myself that I kept back, I thought. I truly loved Rich but even with him, I felt I needed to show that I could cope, show that nothing fazed me. Well Debbie had. She had taken over my thoughts and stressed me out at work and made me feel I had failed her somehow. She was always there niggling at the back of my mind when I should have just been happy - deliriously happy and grateful for my life.

Part of me wanted to run away from the job, but part of me also wanted to fix things and try and make it right. Thinking about Debbie though, made me feel so sick - could I have been more of a friend to her? The trouble was I hadn't felt comfortable with her for ages - she unnerved me and I had no comfort in realising that I had been right to feel wary of her. I had found out from Stella that Pippa had been waiting by my desk to ask me something when Debbie lost it. It made me feel worse that I had asked Pippa to watch out for Debbie, too. This was partly my fault and somehow I had to put things right.

It hit me suddenly and quite forcibly. Actually some stuff just couldn't be fixed. Why try and fix stuff, why not be selfish and do what I wanted – what was right for me, Rich and our baby? Family and friends were what mattered, family and friends. There was so much stuff I couldn't put right with the job centre. No not any more I thought; no more bravado.
"I've changed my mind darling. I'm going to resign. One month's notice that's all I need to give" I looked up and saw Rich smiling broadly and his eyes twinkling.
"At long last" he said "Well done!"

Debbie.

Sometimes I try to think, to function, but it is hard. It is hard to even exist. Various people keep saying they want to help, but I can't connect, I can't understand the questions. I know by remaining disconnected though, that I am protecting myself from something or someone. I am protecting myself from something bad and something very frightening.

They keep asking me to talk about Kate. They call her my other personality. I don't understand why.

Stella.

Lyn and I were round at Pippa's flat, two weeks after she had been discharged from the hospital. Lyn was asking her if she was sure she was ready to come back to work the following week.

"Well you're not going to be there for much longer, are you - so why do you care" she teased.

"We're going to stay in touch though" Lyn replied "That's the main thing."

I wondered if it was the right time to tell them my news. I had been interviewed for a job with Art Support which was a Charity helping youngsters with mental health problems through Art Therapy. I didn't think I had had much chance of getting it. However, I had been offered the job and had accepted straight away. I knew that this was so something I really wanted to do. It would be a challenge and the money wasn't that good but I felt it was just the right thing to do. Make a difference. It was a shame that it would be sort of harder to stay in contact with my friends and I guessed that it meant we may not be so close in the future.

I took a deep breath and then explained about my new job. Initially Pippa was a bit dismissive.

"Well that's right up your street" she said "very Christian of you to go off and help the nut cases."

There was a pause and then with an edge to her voice, she added

"It could be full of weirdoes like Debbie."

"How did she get that screwed up?" I asked.

I knew both Lyn and I felt a bit guilty that we hadn't somehow helped Debbie more. I wasn't sure what Pippa thought. I wasn't sure what we should have done differently, but I remembered that we had all been far friendlier with her, in the first few weeks after starting work together.

"Why did she go for me?" Pippa asked. "To start with, I was thinking I stopped that guy being knifed. I think now she enjoyed hurting me and I felt for ages that she didn't like me much. Well that's her problem, not mine."

Lyn looked like she was going to say something in return but then stopped herself. She cradled her tummy, presumably thinking of her unborn baby.
"Debbie lived with her Mum and Dad, didn't she? I wonder what they make of this. I should have talked to her more about her home life, maybe. I thought that it was particularly me she didn't like - because of having to put her on a warning with all her time off sick. I could never get her to open up; she never really talked about herself."
"That's because she didn't have a life and that's enough about Debbie" Pippa snorted.

I paused whilst thinking about my new job with Art Support.
"You are right though I will be working with people who are screwed up and I bet some of them may be kind of like Debbie and hard to talk to."
"Well" Lyn replied "I guess they are only going to the Art Therapy thingy in the first place because they want to - isn't that meant to be the first step - acknowledging that you've got a problem?"

"My name's Pippa and I am an alcoholic!" Pippa piped up and we all laughed. She then carried on:-
"Seriously though; what was all that stuff Debbie was going on about "Kate" - was that, like, a sign that she's a schizophrenic? Like a Jekyll and Hyde type character? Sorry I forgot - we are not going to talk about Debbie any more. Stella can do her penance for all of us in her next job! We're all moving on. We three must totally stay in touch. All this talk of new beginnings makes me think what Pete was telling me about last night."

"Pete?" I questioned her "You are not back together are you?"
"No way babe" she laughed.
"We're just good friends as it goes, but he was telling me that I should claim compensation for my injury and the stress and all. He reckons I could get quite a pay out! So then I could take some time out, go travelling or whatever. After all, I don't want to end up in the job centre too long, especially as neither of you will be there by the sound of it now. Mind you he thinks they may even keep my job open for me."
"Well, you are definitely keeping your options open; with a job and also maybe Pete to come back to?" I was joking of course but I could see Pippa weighing up the potential.
"Yeah, you've got a point there." She said.

My thoughts turned once again to Debbie. I still couldn't shake off feeling guilty and a bit responsible, somehow, for what had happened. Could we have been better friends with her, could we have been kinder? Why didn't we help her more when she was obviously so troubled? What was going on in her head and what made her flip? I would always wonder but hoped the whole awful experience might help me in my new job. I was so looking forward to it but a bit nervous too.

We were all starting new phases in our lives; but were we really ready to move on? Would we all remember Debbie for the rest of our lives? I knew pretty much that none of us would ever be able to forget what had happened.
"Do you think we should go to the psychiatric hospital and ask to see her?" I asked the others. Somehow I didn't want to use her name.
"No" they both chorused abruptly in reply.

"I don't know that we could help her and it's not like we knew her that well anyway." Lyn said but she couldn't quite raise her eyes to meet mine.
I was somehow relieved but slightly sort of disappointed, too.
"Oh My God - no way" Pippa then added defiantly.
"She's totally not our problem."
I couldn't think of anything to say and so didn't respond. After a brief silence Lyn sighed and then smiled at us.
"Come on then" she cajoled "Let's go out for a drink - I can be the driver for the next six months, you lucky people!"

Kate.

The latest quack tells me that I am here for "a long time."

What a dump. What a fucking awful place.

11052011R00093

Printed in Great Britain
by Amazon.co.uk, Ltd.,
Marston Gate.